MACMILLAN MODERN DRAMATISTS

Macmillan Modern Dramatists
Series Editors: *Bruce King* and *Adele King*

Published titles

Reed Anderson, *Federico Garcia Lorca*
Eugene Benson, *J. M. Synge*
Renate Benson, *German Expressionist Drama*
Normand Berlin, *Eugene O'Neill*
Michael Billington, *Alan Ayckbourn*
John Bull, *New British Political Dramatists*
Denis Calandra, *New German Dramatists*
Neil Carson, *Arthur Miller*
Maurice Charney, *Joe Orton*
Ruby Cohn, *New American Dramatists, 1960–1980*
Bernard F Dukore, *American Dramatists, 1918–1945*
Bernard F Dukore, *Harold Pinter*
Arthur Ganz, *George Bernard Shaw*
James Gibbs, *Wole Soyinka*
Frances Gray, *John Arden*
Julian Hilton, *Georg Büchner*
David L Hirst, *Edward Bond*
Helene Keyssar, *Feminist Theatre*
Bettina L Knapp, *French Theatre 1918–1939*
Charles Lyons, *Samuel Beckett*
Jan McDonald, *The New Drama 1900–1914*
Susan Bassnett-McGuire, *Luigi Pirandello*
Margery Morgan, *August Strindberg*
Leonard C. Pronko, *Eugène Labiche and Georges Feydeau*
Jeanette L Savona, *Jean Genet*
Claude Schumacher, *Alfred Jarry and Guillaume Apollinaire*
Laurence Senelick, *Anton Chekhov*
Theodore Shank, *American Alternative Theatre*
James Simmons, *Sean O'Casey*
David Thomas, *Henrik Ibsen*
Dennis Walder, *Athol Fugard*
Thomas Whitaker, *Tom Stoppard*
Nick Worrall, *Nikolai Gogol and Ivan Turgenev*
Katharine Worth, *Oscar Wilde*

MACMILLAN MODERN DRAMATISTS

WOLE SOYINKA

James Gibbs

MACMILLAN

First published 1986

Published by Higher and Further Education Division
MACMILLAN PUBLISHERS LTD
Houndmills, Basingstoke, Hampshire RG21 2XS
and London
Companies and representatives
throughout the world

Typeset by Type Generation Ltd,
London EC1

Printed in Hong Kong

Gibbs, James
    Wole Soyinka. – (Macmillan modern dramatists)
    1. Soyinka, Wole – Criticism and interpretation
    I. Title
    822   PR9387.9.S6Z/

    ISBN 0-333-30527-2
    ISBN 0-333-30528-0 Pbk

Contents

Acknowledgements

The author wishes to thank his family for support, advice and encouragement; his students and colleagues in Ghana, Malawi and Nigeria for ideas and information, and, finally, Wole Soyinka for creating such remarkable theatre and for permission to quote from the unpublished rehearsal script of *Opera Wonyosi* quoted on page 131.

A note on accents

Yoruba words and names usually appear in Wole Soyinka's books without apostrophes, subscripts or superscripts. I have followed this practice in this study, retaining, as Soyinka does, the accent on *Aké*.

Soyinka's own name is more properly spelt Şoyinka; Ş has a sound roughly equivalent to 'Sh'. For further information on all issues of Yoruba orthography and intonation the reader is referred to R. C. Abraham's *Dictionary of Modern Yoruba*, published by the University of London Press.

List of Plates

The authors and publishers wish to thank copyright holders for permission to reproduce photographs.

For my parents and my wife.

Editors' Preface

The *Macmillan Modern Dramatists* is an international series of introductions to major and significant nineteenth and twentieth century dramatists, movements and new forms of drama in Europe, Great Britain, America and new nations such as Nigeria and Trinidad. Besides new studies of great and influential dramatists of the past, the series includes volumes on contemporary authors, recent trends in the theatre and on many dramatists, such as writers of farce, who have created theatre 'classics' while being neglected by literary criticism. The volumes in the series devoted to individual dramatists include a biography, a survey of the plays, and detailed analysis of the most significant plays, along with discussion, where relevant, of the political, social, historical and theatrical context. The authors of the volumes, who are involved with theatre as playwrights, directors, actors, teachers, and critics, are concerned with the plays as theatre and discuss such matters as performance, character interpretation and staging, along with themes and contexts.

BRUCE KING
ADELE KING

1
Brief Life[1]

Akinwande Oluwole Soyinka, the second child of Samuel
Ayodele and Grace Eniola Soyinka, was born on 13 July
1934. He spent his childhood in Abeokuta, Western
Nigeria; his adolescence and young manhood in Lagos and
Ibadan. For five years, from Autumn 1954 to the end of
1959, he was in England, first reading English at the
University of Leeds and then working in London. In 1960
he returned to Nigeria to do research, write and direct. His
international reputation has grown since the early 1960s,
boosted by the publication of novels, poetry and autobiography as well as by productions of his plays and by his
presence in Europe and America as a lecturer, teacher and
director, sometimes during extended periods of self-exile.

In *Aké* (1981), an account of his first eleven years,
Soyinka has provided vivid portraits of his Yoruba parents
and of the quarter of Abeokuta, Aké, in which he lived with
them. His father, a teacher, moved to Abeokuta from the
Ijebu town of Isara and became headmaster of St Peter's
(Anglican) Primary School, in Aké. His mother, dubbed

1

'Wild Christian' in *Aké*, was born into an Egba family which had played a pioneering role in spreading Christianity through Western Nigeria and had composed music which fused Yoruba and European traditions. She was the grand-daughter of the Rev. J. J. Ransome Kuti, who, in the course of a distinguished career, played a significant role in Yoruba politics, and, in 1905, preached at St Paul's Cathedral. Her uncle, I. O. Ransome Kuti ('Daodu' in *Aké*) was Principal of Abeokuta Grammer School, a public figure who served on the commission which advised the British Government about university education in West Africa. Daodu's wife, Funmilayo, was for many years the major figure in the women's movement in Nigeria and continues to be honoured by progressive forces at home and abroad.

'Wild Christian' herself was a major influence on the young Soyinka. An energetic and extrovert woman of great presence and many accomplishments, she was teacher, performer, political activist and trader. Through her, and her shop opposite the Alake's palace in Abeokuta, Soyinka learnt a vast amount about Yoruba life, particularly about life as it flowed through Aké.

In his autobiography, Soyinka describes not only how he responded to the Yoruba community in which he lived, but also about the very different society which he entered on visits to his father's home-town of Isara. Aké was part of an Egba refugee settlement and had been a major base for European activities in Western Nigeria since 1842. Isara, by contrast, was relatively isolated from the influence of Christianity and had comparatively little contact with white traders. There the young Soyinka met his distinguished Ijebu relatives, including his Grandfather ('Father' in *Aké*) and the Odemo of Isara, a 'volcanic' nationalist of the twenties who had only narrowly missed election to high office.

Soyinka started to attend St Peter's Primary School at a very early age and appears to have moved with ease through the mission primary school system. After St Peter's he spent a year at Abeokuta Grammer School, much of it under the unchallenged authority of his great-uncle, and, in 1946, took up a place at Government College, Ibadan. During the years he spent at that elite institution, he wrote sketches for his house drama group and won prizes with the poems he recited at arts festivals. In 1950, having passed School Certificate, he went to work as a clerk in Lagos. While there he had short stories read on the national broadcasting service and pioneered Nigerian radio drama. He also prepared for entrance to University College, Ibadan, and, in October 1952, began his undergraduate studies, following courses in English, Greek and History at the recently established University College. At the College, he played leading roles in productions, co-founded a fraternity (The Pyrates), edited a student publication (*The Eagle*), and continued with his creative writing. After taking and passing the Intermediate Arts Examination, he entered, in October 1954, the University of Leeds where he began to read for an Honours Degree in the School of English.

At Leeds the twenty-year-old Nigerian acted with the University's Theatre Group, had short stories published in the student literary magazine, sang in a rag revue, took an interest in politics and encountered the prejudices of some of the British. After being awarded an Upper Second Class Honours degree in 1957, he began to work on an MA, but his real interest appears to have been in writing and, around this time, he began drafting two important plays, *The*

Swamp Dwellers and *The Lion and the Jewel*. The second of these was read by Anne Piper on behalf of the Royal Court Theatre in Sloane Square, London. As a result of her enthusiasm and the interest of others at the Court, the young playwright was encouraged to become involved in the activities of that theatre.

Soyinka moved to London during 1958 and, apart from his work at the theatre, taught, broadcast and wrote. He also directed a group, the Nigeria Drama Group, in *The Swamp Dwellers* (December 1958).[2] The following year, as part of his involvement with the Court, he wrote a song, 'Long time, Bwana' – an expression of the feelings of the Kenyan people, which formed part of an evening of largely improvized material about British colonial violence in Kenya. During November (1959), he directed an 'Evening' of his own work at the theatre; the programme included poetry and songs which revealed his interest in Black American styles, and dramatic pieces, particularly *The Invention*, which showed his loathing of racism, and, in particular, of Apartheid. At this time, he evolved a clear perception of his future as a playwright who employed the idiom of African art to create a theatre which was responsive to contemporary events.

On January 1st 1960, the year in which the country was to become independent, Soyinka returned to Nigeria and took up a two-year Rockefeller research studentship which enabled him to study drama in West Africa. The rapid pace of Nigerianisation during the late fifties had lifted his contemporaries from school and college days into positions of influence, particularly in the radio corporation and the newly established Western Nigerian Television Service. The Students' Dramatic Society at University College was looking for actors and for scripts by local writers; editors were anxious to fill local magazines and journals with verse and literary criticism by Nigerians. Soyinka joined, and soon became the leader of, an intensely creative community of young artists. During 1960, *The Swamp Dwellers* was broadcast; Soyinka gave radio talks and contributed to broadcast discussions. He also completed two new radio plays, *Camwood on the Leaves* and *The Tortoise*; a television play, entitled *My Father's Burden*, and a stage play, *The Trials of Brother Jero*, all of which were produced. On the campus of University College, Ibadan, he sang at a Music Society concert and played Yang Sun in a production of Bertolt Brecht's *The Good Woman of Setzuan*.

Soyinka's major undertaking during the year was a production, in Lagos and Ibadan, of *A Dance of the Forests*, a revised version of an earlier anti-Apartheid piece, *The Dance of the African Forest*. For the production of *A Dance* he drew together a group of friends who were experienced amateur actors and actresses and with them formed the '1960 Masks'. The group's first stage production was addressed to Nigeria at the time of Independence (1 October) and deliberately challenged expectations concerning the future of the country and assumptions about the form Nigerian theatre in English would take. For some this complex and sometimes confusing play revealed Soyinka as an *enfant terrible*, a writer who delighted in shocking and bewildering his audience. For others he emerged as an independent thinker with numerous theatrical skills and a vaulting ambition. The ambivalent relationship between the Nigerian public and Wole Soyinka had begun.

No major new plays appeared from his hand in 1961, partly, it appears, because much of his creative energy went into writing scripts for a weekly radio-series, *Broke-Time Bar*, which ran for many months. The scripts for the series have never been published and Soyinka's involvement with this popular series has sometimes, unfortunately, been overlooked. He ceased to write *Broke-Time Bar* when the broadcasting authorities resisted his introduction of trenchant social and political comment – one of several brushes between the writer and the establishment.

During 1961 a commitment to prepare a trilogy of plays for television, *The House of Banijegi* was only partly realised. *The Night of the Hunted* was transmitted but the other two episodes remained unproduced and, possibly, in draft form only. During the year, Soyinka began to live on a larger map: he attended conferences in Italy and America and his poems were published in Sweden. He was also involved in plans to make a film about Nigerian culture for Esso: in due course this was released as 'Culture in Transition' with Soyinka as presenter and with an abbreviated version of *The Strong Breed*.

During 1962, Soyinka contributed regularly to Nigerian controversies through the press. He manipulated the media so as to ensure that space was available for him to express his views and so that he could make an impact on his countrymen. In the course of the year he attacked Negritude, contradicted a leading newspaper columnist, Peter Enahoro, jeered at expatriate literary critics and complained about the censorship of the press. He also took up a post as lecturer in English at University College, Ife, and defined his position as a literary critic in talks and essays. His employment as lecturer did not, however, last long: a political crisis developed in the Western Region and was exploited by the Federal Government in order to silence opposition voices. When the University College gave way to political pressure, Soyinka resigned.

At this time of violence, victimisation, repression and censorship, when the press and the radio were both increasingly under pressure from the government, Soyinka turned to drama and specifically to the satirical revue form to make known his feelings. He wrote sketches for *The Republican*, which was mounted by the 1960 Masks towards the end of 1963 and which was revived with new material as *The (New) Republican* during March 1964. In the middle of 1964, with a strike in progress and talk of revolution in the air, he advocated and worked for a people's uprising. But the moment passed and he turned to a project, a season of plays, which advanced his plans for the development of drama by bringing together the Nigerian theatre in English with the Nigerian theatre in Yoruba. His contribution to the programme consisted of *The Lion and the Jewel*, which he directed with a group of young enthusiasts, several of whom hoped to become professional performers and joined a new drama group, 'Orisun Theatre'.

Political violence returned to the streets of Western Nigeria during 1965 with renewed intensity, and in March, at a time when ministers were being murdered and party arsonists were active, Soyinka bravely produced a new revue, *Before the Blackout*, another onslaught on opportunist politicians, corrupt time-servers and cynical manipulators. The only item which has survived in the repertoires of African schools and colleges is *Childe Internationale*, the very effective final sketch from the revue.

Against a background of national crisis, Soyinka produced his first major play of the mid-sixties, *Kongi's Harvest*, in the Federal Palace Hotel, Lagos, during August, 1965. The following month, he was in London to read his long poem 'Idanre' as part of the Commonwealth Arts Festival, to advise on the production of his metaphysical-satirical play, *The Road*, which was being presented on the fringe of the Festival at the Theatre Royal, Stratford East, and to take part in recording *The Detainee*, a political piece which he had written for the BBC. The radio play, which has not been published, warns against the rise of one-party states and of dictators; it was broadcast to a large part of the African continent. In addition to these new plays, 1965 saw Soyinka's appointment as a senior lecturer at the University of Lagos and the publication of a major novel, *The Interpreters*.

Soon after his return to Nigeria from London, elections, accompanied by violence, were held in Western Nigeria. Chief S.L. Akintola was declared the winner, but, instead of his taped victory address to the region, listeners to Ibadan radio-station heard part of a tape which began 'This is the Voice of Free Nigeria' and went on to advise Akintola and his 'crew of renegades' to quit the country.[3] This pirate broadcast was variously described as a prank, a political protest and a rehearsal for a *coup d'état*. A warrant was issued for Soyinka's arrest. In the trial following his arrest, a trial which could have brought a severe sentence and which occasionally bordered on farce, Soyinka pleaded 'not guilty'. Eventually he was acquitted on what some regard as a technicality and jubilant supporters carried him shoulder-high from the court. The episode had placed him at the centre of public interest for several weeks.

The twenty months between Soyinka's acquittal and his re-arrest during August 1967 in connection with the Civil War were momentous ones for Nigeria. There was a coup by radical and progressive officers; a counter-coup which brought Yakubu Gowon to power; the secession of Biafra, and the drift into civil war. During this period, Soyinka's creativity appears to have flowed into poetry, productions and essays. His verse included 'Massacre October '66' and 'For her who Rejoiced'; he directed *Home Again* by Lindsay Barrett, a West Indian resident in Nigeria, and *The Crucible* by Arthur Miller. His critical writing from these months is particularly revealing and influential: *And After the Narcissist?*, *Of Power and Change* and *The Fourth Stage* were published or submitted for publication. Significant as these have proved to be, it was his contributions to the Nigerian press which had the more immediate and dramatic results: through the press he campaigned for appropriate peace initiatives to stem the rising tide of violence in the North and for a cease-fire in the war against Biafra.[4] His call for a cease-fire was coupled with a ferocious indictment of 'patriots and other sordid racketeers', and this attack, together with federal embarrassment at military reverses in the Mid-West, may have been partly responsible for his arrest and for his detention without trial.

For twenty-seven months, until October 1969, Soyinka was detained, mostly in solitary confinement in Kaduna Prison, an experience he has described in his prison notes, *The Man Died*. On his release he carried from prison a certain amount of poetry, some of which he had written with a quill and cell-manufactured 'ink' between the lines of printed books, and with material for plays and a novel. He immediately took up the post of director of the school of drama at Ibadan. He took over a production of *Kongi's Harvest* which Dapo Adelugba, then on the faculty of the school, had begun, and gave it an anti-military, anti-Gowon slant. During 1970, he prepared a shooting-script of the same play for a film company and, in March and April, acted Kongi before the cameras.

By July 1970, Soyinka had obtained sufficient support from the University of Ibadan to establish a department of theatre arts and a theatre arts company. On behalf of himself and the acting group, he accepted an invitation to rehearse and perform a play at the Eugene O'Neill Center, at Waterford, Connecticut. He took with him an incomplete script of *Madmen and Specialists*, some of which he may have written while in prison, and during rehearsals at Waterford he reworked and added to the text, which was eventually presented at the Center and in local black communities by a cast which included several who had been close to Soyinka for many years. The following March, a slightly revised version of *Madmen* was presented in Ibadan and then on the eve of the release of the film version of *Kongi's Harvest*, Soyinka left 'Gowon's Nigeria' for what he intended should be a 'brief exile', largely in Europe.

The 'brief exile' lasted, in fact, for nearly five years and took him to many parts of the world. It drew from him several lectures and essays, *The Man Died*, a compilation of African poetry, a second novel (*Season of Anomy*) and three important, published plays: *Jero's Metamorphosis, The Bacchae of Euripides* and *Death and the King's Horseman*. The first of these plays is, in certain respects, in the tradition of the sketches written during the sixties, but it is longer, more elaborate and more pessimistic. The second was written to fulfil a commission from the National Theatre in London, but, since it is a radical re-writing of a play Soyinka had long wanted to work on, it is not in any sense hack-work. *Horseman*, which was written while the author was an overseas fellow at Churchill College, Cambridge, was based on an historical event which had been suggested as providing a suitable base for dramatic treatment over ten years earlier.

In 1974, Soyinka left Europe for Accra, Ghana, to become editor of Africa's leading intellectual magazine, *Transition*. He used the publication, which he soon renamed *Ch'Indaba*, to support socialist revolutionary movements on the continent and to attack tyrants, such as Francisco Macias Nguema, Jean-Bedel Bokassa and Idi Amin. He also prepared his Cambridge play and lectures for the press and became involved in a debate with those who regarded him as a reactionary presence in the drive to 'decolonise' African literature. While in Accra and in order to protect the interests of writers and to campaign for human rights, Soyinka joined with Dennis Brutus and others in the inauguration of the Union of Writers of African Peoples. He was elected Secretary General of the Union.

Gowon was overthrown in July 1975 in a coup which brought Murtala Mohammad to power at the head of a military government with which Soyinka felt able to work. The self-exiled writer returned home during December to a warm welcome from his family and those who had supported him in his acrimonious dispute with Gowon. In January, he took up a professorship at the University of Ife, and became, in some respects, allied to the establishment. The alliance was, however, an uneasy one, especially after February when Mohammad was assassinated during an attempted putsch and Olusegun Obasanjo succeeded as head of state.

In the Nigeria to which Soyinka returned social problems were more pressing, inequalities of wealth more glaring and evidence of political corruption more blatant than ever before. The 'season of anomy' was the result, partly at least, of the Civil War and the oil-boom economy which had come with the oil price-rises of the early seventies. In these altered circumstances, a new generation of critics and writers was demanding that the theatre should contribute to positive social thinking and purposeful communal action. Soyinka became a focus for their interest since, in addition to his position as professor, he took on certain responsibilities at a state level for improving road safety and became involved, for a time, in the administration of the Second Black and African Festival of Arts and Culture (Festac), which was held during January 1977.

Soyinka's first production after his return was of *Death and the King's Horseman* (December 1976). This was followed a year later by a far more committed piece, one which established a dominant direction in his subsequent work, *Opera Wonyosi*, an adaptation of Bertolt Brecht's *Threepenny Opera*. This attacked, often in song, several African tyrants and many of the values of oil-boom Nigeria. It was a large-scale production, designed to make an impact in a well-equipped theatre-building. When plans to mount it in Lagos were thwarted by reactionary forces, Soyinka formed a new group, the Guerrilla Theatre Unit of the University of Ife, and began writing playlets for presentation in streets, market-places and lorry-parks. Two of these 'hit and run' pieces, under the title *Before the Blow-out*, followed the political manoeuvring of some of the crooks and charlatans introduced in *Opera Wonyosi* and commented on events surrounding the preparations for the return to civilian rule. During 1979, Soyinka directed and acted in *The Biko Inquest*, an edited version of the proceedings in the South African courts following the death, in police custody, of black consciousness leader Steve Biko. The production was a clinical exposé of the inhumanity and deceit in far-off South Africa, but the play was not allowed to become in any sense escapist. All the parts were taken by black actors, and the piece was obviously relevant to the Nigeria in which police brutality and lack of integrity in the judicial system were commonplace.

During September and October 1979, the period of elections and the return to civilian rule, Soyinka directed *Horseman* in Chicago. The production was very well received and was transferred to Washington DC: it raised Soyinka's reputation in the American theatre to a new level. Although he left rehearsals, the production and the

United States to make several visits to Nigeria during the run up to the elections it may be that the Chicago production prevented his influencing political events at a sensitive time.

The announcement that Shehu Shagari had been elected President of Nigeria as a result of the October election raised cries of protest from the opposition parties. Many thought Shagari owed his position to an unacceptable interpretation of the paragraphs in the Constitution regarding the percentage of votes required to elect a President.

Soyinka had some links with members of the opposition Unity Party of Nigeria (UPN) and accepted the chairmanship of the Oyo State Road Safety Corps (OSRSC). He indicated that he was attracted to the radical socialism of the People's Redemption Party (PRP), but he never joined that Party, preferring to consider himself a 'self-suspended member' and to challenge the attitudes and actions of some of its leaders.

During 1980, Soyinka was deeply involved in the activities of the Road Safety Corps and in the life of the University of Ife, working closely with his friend and hunting companion, Tunji Aboyade, the Vice-Chancellor. In December, he delivered his inaugural lecture, a professorial obligation, on the topic *The Critic and Society: Barthes, Leftocracy and Other Mythologies*. The paper constitutes a major statement in his continuing debate with his critics in Nigeria, particularly those of the Left.

Part of 1981 was spent as a visiting professor at Yale University, where he anticipated directing a new work, *A Play of Giants*, 'a fantasia on the Aminian theme'. However, distractions from the media and commitments in Nigeria made this impossible. In fact, Soyinka returned home from Yale so frequently, and made such an impact during these visits, that some of his colleagues at the

University of Ife, were not aware that he was a visiting professor at Yale during that period! When he returned full-time to Ife, his energies were stretched by his significant role in campus matters. Issues confronting the administration over this period included the collapse of a hall of residence, acute water shortages, chronic overcrowding in student rooms, a ritual murder, the deaths of four students while taking part in a peaceful demonstration and scurrilous attacks on the Vice-Chancellor.

It was, however, a national issue which prompted a play and the result was another piece of political street theatre. Provoked by the racketeering and profiteering connected with the importation and distribution of rice, he wrote *Rice Unlimited*, a brief sketch which was presented in the heart of Lagos as part of a demonstration.

During January 1982, Soyinka launched *Aké* in Abeokuta. The autobiography of his first eleven and half years, begun in Accra and completed after his return to Nigeria in 1976, was his major literary achievement of the late seventies and early eighties. Quite obviously a dramatist's autobiography, with dialogue and characters ready for the stage, *Aké* is also, though less obviously, the work of a man under attack for being 'too European' in the eyes of some of his countrymen. The vivid, amusing, and deeply felt account was greeted with enthusiasm by reviewers and readers in the UK and, particularly, in the US. In Nigeria the author took advantage of the launching of the book to continue his attack on Shagari's government. As part of his jeremiad, he listed what he described as the 'achievements' of the ruler: Shuguba's deportation; the despoilation of the country's wealth; the Bakolori Massacre; the subversion of the Kano state government; the destruction of the offices of *The Triumph* newspaper; the 'butchering' of Bala Mohammed; the storming of an elected legislature, and the

deaths at the hands of policemen of students, athletes and
Youth Corpers. The statement, with others like it and *Rice
Unlimited*, made Soyinka's one of the clearest voices
opposing Shagari.

As if to show that he was still capable of working on
material that deepened awareness rather than simply
sharpened anger about specific issues, Soyinka staged his
early radio-play *Camwood on the Leaves* at the National
Theatre in Lagos during March and April (1982). Operat-
ing on yet another level, he delivered, on 18 August at
Stratford-on-Avon, a lecture entitled *Shakespeare and the
Living Dramatist*. At that time he was working on a play
concerned with the influence of 'metaphysicians and parapsychologists' in Nigeria. This became a half-hour radio
play, *Die Still Rev. Dr. Godspeak!*, which was broadcast in
the African Service of the BBC during December, and a
full-length play, *Requiem for a Futurologist*, which he
directed and toured during the opening months of 1983.

Requiem made fun of the credulous and exposed apos-
tates in much the same spirit as *The Trials of Brother Jero*
had done. It was sometimes accompanied on tour by the
agit-prop sketches which followed *Rice Unlimited*: namely
Festac 77, The Green Revolution, Ethical Revolution and
Abuja, known collectively as *Priority Projects*. These used
spectacle, simple dialogue, pungent lyrics and attractive
music to draw attention to the corruption, mismanagement
and hypocrisy in the country. In order to communicate with
his countrymen even more widely, Soyinka had the songs
which accompanied the sketches recorded and they were
released on the 'flip-side' of a record entitled *Unlimited
Liability Company* during July 1983. The title song, a
chanson à clef, concerned a badly run 'company' led by a
'chairman' who had neither the will nor the ability to
control his corrupt directors. The record was sold, broad-

cast and transmitted in the weeks before the August national elections. Very shortly before election day, another Soyinka song, 'Take the First Step', joined his anthems for the opposition parties in the campaign to beat Shagari and his National Party of Nigeria (NPN) at the polls.

There was violence during the elections and turmoil in some states when the official results, which awarded Shagari a second victory, were announced. Soyinka flew to London and, through the British press and on the African Service of the BBC, described the background to the elections, the manipulation of the Western press and the distortions in the official results. He predicted that there would be 'a coup or a civil war or a combination of both'.

Despite a report that the Nigerian police wanted to question him in connection with arms purchases (shades of 1967), a five million naira libel action for comments in *The Man Died* and the persecution of those who had broadcast his songs, Soyinka returned to Ife. He was there when, on 31 December 1983, Shagari was overthrown by the *Coup* which brought Mohammadu Buhari to power. The new leader indicated that he and his colleagues had seized power because of the extent of the corruption in the civilian administration. The marketing of rice and the construction of the new capital at Abuja were cited as particular examples of corruption. The coup-makers justified their intervention by pointing to the very abuses which Soyinka had, with others, been attacking.

While appreciating the anti-corruption stance of the Buhari regime, Soyinka regarded some actions with suspicion. He was quick to condemn the sweeping ban on all political parties and expressed concern about the 'over-enthusiasm' of some of the military governors.

During February 1984, Justice Ademola-Johnson handed down his judgement in a case brought by Femi Okunnu for damages over *The Man Died*. Ademola-Johnson praised the industry and patriotism evidenced by the prison notes but upheld part of Okunnu's case. He granted the plaintiff an injuction restraining the Nigerian publishers, the University of Lagos, from selling the book. For the first time since its publication, *The Man Died* was banned.

During the run-up to the election in 1983 and into the early months of 1984, Soyinka worked on a film, *Blues for a Prodigal*. Initially, in Soyinka's words, 'a straightforward propaganda film . . . an almost unambiguous call to arms', the approach was modified after the December coup. This finished film retains the original story about a student seduced into recruiting for a political party on a university campus, but it is not as heavily political as was originally intended.[5] In May his production of *The Road* opened in Chicago and in December *A Play of Giants* was premiered at the University of Yale.

2
Sources and Influences

On one of his holiday visits to Isara, the young Soyinka went through a rite designed to strengthen and protect him. Besides this intense, individual experience, he shared with the community in the New Year Festivals which attracted the scattered 'sons and daughters' of the town and which lasted for several days. At the heart of Yoruba New Year celebrations are, characteristically, purification rites; in celebrating them, innovations, as long as they conform to Yoruba aesthetic principles, are permissible, indeed they are encouraged. The pattern of the festival, the concern with communal purification and the eclecticism of the celebration were important for the growing playwright and they provide an example of the kind of inspiration Soyinka found in his African background.

From *Aké*, it is clear that Soyinka was fascinated from an early age by the god Ogun, whom his mother dismissed as 'the pagan's devil' but whom his grandfather in Isara regarded with great respect. Over the years, Soyinka has returned again and again to this figure of Yoruba cosmology, the patron deity of hunters and soldiers, of all who work

18

with metal, a just god, an inventive pioneering spirit, an artist and creator who is capable of ferocious acts of destructive violence. Many stories are told about him, and Soyinka, who responds deeply to myths, has found some of them particularly meaningful. One which he has studied in search of an insight into the Yoruba attitude to creativity and innovation tells how Ogun visited earth before the other gods and discovered the secret of smelting iron. When the gods descended as a group at Ile-Ife, they found themselves separated from mankind by a 'chthonic realm' or 'primordial marsh', to use terms employed by Soyinka. Bold Ogun, armed with an iron axe, launched himself into 'the abyss' on a mission of reconciliation and made a 'road' in order to unite gods with human beings.

Another myth which Soyinka has found particularly revealing concerns the 'terrible slaughter at Ajo Oriki'. Ogun, the narrative relates, had been made King of Ire, but one day, perhaps drunk on palm-wine, he slew many of his friends. Festivals in honour of Ogun are celebrated in Yorubaland and in the New World; they sometimes involve the sacrifice of a dog or a procession-dance with metal tipped palm-fronds. During this century Ogun has become, in Soyinka's words, 'the primal motor mechanic': he is the god of drivers who often swerve violently in order to hit stray dogs, to sacrifice them to Ogun lest he demand 'heavier meat', and who hold festivals during which masked figures dance through the streets.

Since, at least the early fifties, Soyinka has pondered the significance of Ogun's duality, his combination of creativity and destructiveness. In several essays, particularly *The Fourth Stage*, he has played Aristotle to his own Sophocles, Nietzsche to his own Wagner and G. Wilson Knight to his own Shakespeare: he has developed a theory of drama based on a subjective analysis of Ogun festivals which illuminates the tragic vision embodied in his plays. He has described Ogun as his 'patron deity'.

There is no religious orthodoxy in Yorubaland and in going to Isara, Soyinka was visiting an area which regarded Agemo as a major deity. The annual Agemo festivals, for which the deity wears a mask topped with a carving of a chameleon ('alagemo'), involve acrobatic dances, the performance of rituals at specific places, processions and spectacular transformations wrought by means of cunningly designed costumes. Agemo is also, like Ogun, concerned with roads. During his ceremonial processions he has right of way and may on no account be hindered as he moves from shrine to shrine. Ideas connected with the deity and the conventions which shape his festivals provide a background to *The Road* and a key to its structure.

Soyinka was intrigued by the theatrical conventions, idioms, meanings and themes of such deities and festivals. In a conference paper on *The 'African Approach to Drama'* (1960), he indicated his acquaintance with numerous Nigerian rites and his awareness of the theatrical qualities of many of them.[1] He argued that worshippers often processed from shrine to shrine, performed rituals, beat out rhythms and danced dances ignorant of the historical event, legend or myth which lay behind the celebration. The rites demanded, he argued, an intellectual submission, a willingness to respond to changing moods and tempos. In the festivals which he described, such as the Passion Play of Obatala, about the deity responsible for creating people, and the Oshun Festival at Oshogbo, there were theatrical conventions which could be used by the playwright anxious to write plays which drew inspiration from local rites. The festivals were created around juxtapositions, contrasts and comparisons rather than character or narrative – which loom so large in the European tradition of drama.

Behind several of the festivals which Soyinka found most useful in his play construction was the theme associated with the New Year Festival: desire for purification. Individuals and communities, he observed, felt the need to purge themselves of blood-guilt after killing an enemy, kinsman or animal, or of unburdening themselves of the evil which had accumulated over a period. Sometimes the purgation took the form of an expiatory dance around the body of the victim. Sometimes, as in Ife, it involved selecting a 'carrier', a stranger or a retarded individual, who was 'prepared', led through the streets and then expelled from the town bearing the curses and the evil of the community. On occasions, as in some communities of the Niger Delta, the role of the carrier was inherited and the cleansing of the community, the 'placing' of the evil in a small boat which the carrier launched on the out-going tide, was conducted with dignity and a high degree of stylization. In celebrations with a related purpose, masquerades, such as Eyo Adimu, performed the function of the carrier. In others effigies were dragged through the streets of certain towns and beaten. In Abeokuta these effigies had become known as 'Judases', evidence of a mingling of religious traditions. Soyinka, who was surrounded by Christian influences in the Parsonage, has shown a great sensitivity to cultural coincidences. In *The Strong Breed*, for instance, there is a mingling and contrasting of Yoruba purification rites and deliberate references to Christian doctrines; the play stresses similarities between Yoruba concepts of self-sacrifice and Judaeo-Christian ideas. For that play, as for many others, Soyinka sought inspiration in Yoruba theatre traditions, festivals and rituals.

In Abeokuta, as the Judas effigies indicated, Soyinka was surrounded by evidence of syncretism, of continuity and change. He was impressed by the ability of the people he grew up among to accommodate new ideas, realities and technologies within an elastic world-view. On the first page of *Aké*, he refers to *egungun*, which he describes as an 'ancestral masquerade'. Annual *egungun* festivals were held which involved vigils, the sacrifice of animals on the graves of ancestors, dances at the palaces of *obas* or chiefs, and processions with masquerades around the town. The young Soyinka learnt of the *egungun* of a District officer that had appeared some years before – clearly the costume-makers and impersonators of Abeokuta had responded creatively to distinctive new presences in the community. The masqueraders were not bound by a narrow sense that only the ancestors of particular local families could appear in processions. Their example provided the young play-maker with precedents for an eclectic approach.

The Abeokuta of the thirties and forties played host to a centuries-old tradition of Yoruba travelling theatre, an off-shoot of the *egungun* masquerade, the Alarinjo.[2] As a boy Soyinka learnt about the masque-dramaturges of this convention, the *egungun opidan*, who were responsible for the productions which were offered in open spaces such as that which lay just across the road from Wild Christian's shop. The productions included acrobatic dances and dance dramas, and involved representative figures as well as recognisable individuals. Dances incorporated a high degree of stylisation and a formal structure, which was sometimes superficially regarded as repetitive but was, in fact, a series of variations on a pattern. A particularly popular piece was *The Masque of the Bride*, which was frequently used to bring a performance to an end. In the closing moments of that masque, the Bride, danced by a man, adjusts his clothes to reveal a baby secured to his back and then processes through the streets. The conventions and concerns of the masque, including the attitude to

22

characterization, the use of stylized gesture and dance, the emphasis on fertility and the procession off as a means of concluding a performance, provided Soyinka with an indigenous form on which he could draw in his declared aim of combining African performance idioms with the 'European' traditions of dialogue drama. The time Soyinka spent in his mother's shop was, it seems, an important part of his education: it provided points of contact with the market life which often appears in his plays and an introduction to Yoruba masquerade theatre.

While the masquerade tradition was basically an indigenous form which was constantly interacting with a changing community, a theatrical development was taking place in which the indigenous and imported elements were more evenly balanced. The soil in which this grew was partly Yoruba town life, partly Christian worship and partly the concert and theatre traditions which had taken root in Lagos from the nineteenth century. An epoch-marking event in the evolution of this form took place in 1944 when Hubert Ogunde, the son of a Baptist minister, produced what he called 'a grand native-air opera', in effect a stage show, entitled *The Garden of Eden and the Throne of God*. At the invitation of the Alake of Aké, the production was put on at Centenary Hall. It was followed by *Africa and God*, which, by presenting 'the music and dances of Yorubaland before the advent of missionaries', provided an obvious opportunity to use local material. Ogunde recruited performers and pioneered a tradition of professional Yoruba theatre which, from the mid-forties, made drama a major vehicle for nationalism and provided numerous examples of how Yoruba performance conventions, myths, legends and music could be presented within the two or three hour 'traffic of the stage'.[3] Soyinka has worked with Yoruba travelling theatre groups over the years, he has promoted their productions and learnt both from them and from the vigorous comic theatres, such as that of Moses Olaiya with its combination of satire and slap-stick, which developed in their wake. It is no coincidence that Soyinka's plays make extensive use of the setting which this theatre movement grew, for the worship of independent African churches is often intensely theatrical.

Even without going to Isara, his mother's shop or Centenary Hall, Soyinka moved in a world in which expressions of drama were near at hand, for the performing arts were close to the surface of life in the parsonage. In *Aké*, he describes how his mother performed impromptu dances when teaching, how his father told him bed-time stories and sang bed-time songs, how he had a receptive audience for his imitations of unpopular visitors, how he crept out of bed to listen to the stories told by Ijebu relatives camping in the parsonage compound, how a neighbour's daughter was humiliated by songs for wetting her bed, and how the verses of the Oro chanters were wafted from the Alake's palace into his room. Given this environment it is not surprising that Soyinka's theatre should, at its most characteristic, employ dance, music, song, gesture and symbol as well as dialogue.

Indications of the ways in which Soyinka transformed the raw material of the life which surrounded him during his youth into his plays are provided by almost all his works. He has indicated, for instance, that Amope, the cloth seller who is determined to collect a debt in *The Trials*, has some qualities in common with his mother, Wild Christian, and that the character is also representative, in some respects, of 'the Yoruba petty-trader type'. In Amope, as in many other of his most successful characters, Soyinka portrayed the quality of a group through an individual. In play after play he has drawn on the world of the parsonage, on members of his family and on the wider Yoruba society he got to know. He observed the effect of wealth on family life and used his observations in *The Swamp Dwellers*. He watched ill-dressed school teachers and noted the success of resilient elders who married young wives and used his notes on the conflict as background for *The Lion and the Jewel*. He drew on his recollections of the lorry-parks of post-war Abeokuta for *The Road*, and on rumours of war-time explosions in Lagos harbour for an exchange in *Death and the King's Horseman*. The book of childhood memories indicates that he moved in a world of tremendous variety and got to know an extraordinary range of people, from powerful title-holders to vulnerable, mentally unstable, denizens of the market place. He clearly relished the variety and diversity of humanity, and, from childhood, enjoyed creating characters based on people he had encountered.

Beginning school does not seem to have been a traumatic experience for Soyinka. In *Aké*, he described how one day he followed his elder sister, Dupe, across the compound from the parsonage and slipped into the classroom. In many ways, his home life and his school life complemented each other. His father was headmaster of his primary school; English was one of the languages spoken at home as well as one of those taught at school; the rediffusion set and his father's library reinforced some of the lessons he was learning on the benches in class. In school Yoruba lessons he read D. O. Fagunwa's Yoruba novels which contained folk material such as he had heard at bed-time story-telling sessions and evangelical messages such as he had encountered at church and at his mother's knee. Although the school provided much that was strange and new it also

25

contained the familiar: here, once again, was evidence to the young writer of continuity and change, similarity and difference.

After five years Soyinka left the Anglican primary school with its inevitable emphasis on Biblical stories and Christian teaching for the Grammar School which was a centre for Egba nationalism. The musical tradition at that school was particularly strong, and the principal, Daodu, himself a composer, encouraged the cultivation of musical talents. Partly due to this, Soyinka has a highly developed musical sense, with a facility for writing songs in Yoruba and for composing. Government College, which he moved to in 1946, was, by contrast, a colonial institution which took an interest in marking events connected with British royalty and had a strong tradition of athletics, swimming and cricket. However, it was not, as *Aké* might be taken to suggest, staffed exclusively, or even predominently, by Englishmen in the post-war period. There were Nigerian nationalists on the staff and the vigorous political debate which was going forward in the country during the late forties was echoed in the school.

Samuel Ayodele Soyinka wanted his son Wole to become a medical practitioner, but the young Soyinka's inclinations lay elsewhere. He read voraciously, particularly novels and biographies, and he began to express himself creatively in verse and drama. His decision to leave school, his interest in writing for radio and his decision to do Arts subjects at University College, Ibadan, show his creative tendencies, his initiative and his single-mindedness.

The radio plays and short stories he wrote while in Lagos are not available, but they are presumably apprentice works; he described the playlets as 'seven-tenths imitation of the women's comedy hour'. From the poem and the short story he published while an undergraduate at Ibadan,

'Thunder into Storm' and 'Keffi's Birthday Treat', it is clear that he was far better at handling narrative than verse.

At University College during the early fifties, Soyinka found himself in the company of an elite group drawn from all over the country undergoing a colonial education while burning with the nationalist fervour which their generation of Nigerians felt. During his two years at the college, he deepened and broadened his awareness of European literary and dramatic traditions by studying a syllabus which included work by Austen, Tennyson, Newman, Hardy, Shaw and Shakespeare. He began to learn Greek and he studied history, not African history since the colonial education system hardly recognised that Africa had any history. He took the roles of Tobias in *Tobias and the Angel* and of Dick Dudgeon in *The Devil's Disciple*, and he earned high praise. His contributions to the student newspapers at Ibadan provide evidence of his wit, rhetorical style and concern for individual rights.

As an undergraduate at Leeds (1954–57), Soyinka found himself in a creative community of students and in touch with inspiring teachers. During his first three years he became very familiar with British and European dramatic traditions. He had opportunities to see many plays in production, and some of these were in a tradition which struck a particularly responsive chord, the tradition of the *Commedia dell'arte*. These Italian plays, often in translations by the head of the Leeds Italian department, Frederick May, involved partly masked characters representing regional types in farcical, sometimes improvised, sequences. The plots frequently revolved around marriage, greed and the attempts of the senile to thwart young love – themes which Soyinka had encountered in the Yoruba masque theatre.

Two of the courses Soyinka took at Leeds were taught by

a renowned scholar-actor-author, G. Wilson Knight, who became a personal friend. Knight's World Drama course covered tragedy and comedy from the Greeks to the twentieth century, and his Ibsen course covered all the Norwegian dramatist's major plays. Knight was concerned with the origins and the theory of drama and with the totality and theatricality of texts. He saw 'great drama' as more ceremony than entertainment, as a rite in which actors and audience share in the formal unfurling of some deeply significant pattern, and believed it was possible for the dead to communicate with the living. His book *The Golden Labyrinth* includes an acknowledgement of the influence of one of Soyinka's essays and there are moments during the subsequent careers of the two men when their mutual respect is apparent. Soyinka emerged from his drama studies at Leeds, partly thanks to Knight, intimately acquainted with European dramatic traditions. Several of his plays contain creative responses to aspects of that tradition, and Knight's teaching of it, others quote from work which he had read, acted in or seen.

At Stratford-on-Avon during 1983, Soyinka acknowledged that he had been influenced by everything he had read. While in some senses a discouragement to those making specific comparisons, this alerts us to regard Soyinka as self-consciously working in a literary tradition. He is a writer who is convinced of the validity of re-employing existing material. Like European playwrights from Sophocles to Shakespeare to Brecht, he regards eclecticism as a right, maintaining that it is what an artist does with borrowed material that is important; what or how much he takes is not significant. During the seventies, Soyinka wrote two adaptations and during the eighties he has gone to Jonathan Swift for a theatrical situation. While these moves reflect a shift of emphasis, they do not, as might at first appear, represent a radical departure: Soyinka's work has always drawn on existing material in both the Yoruba and European traditions.

In *The Swamp Dwellers*, which was written at Leeds, Soyinka worked within a tradition of poetic-naturalistic treatments of peasant societies confronted by new values and by disruptive social forces. This tradition is illustrated by the work of Anton Chekhov, by Luigi Pirandello's *The Life that I Gave You*, Gerhart Hauptmann's *Before Dawn*, and, most significantly for Soyinka's play, by J. M. Synge's *The Shadow of the Glen*. Soyinka has acknowledged the impact on his writing of Synge's use of English, and it is clear that, he found the endeavours of Irish writers, particularly Synge and Sean O'Casey, to use local material and find an English idiom for their Irish dramas particularly inspiring. *The Swamp Dwellers* is the one play in which, to use a distinction established by T.S. Eliot, Soyinka borrowed rather than stole from the European tradition; it should be seen as apprentice work.

The Lion and the Jewel, also a Leeds play, represents a dialogue with the European tradition of comedy and of plays about impotence from Terence's *Eunuch* to Ben Jonson's *Volpone* and William Wycherley's *The Country Wife*. However, it employs a dramatic convention substantially different from those found in the European tradition and presents a view of an old suitor quite unlike that of conventional European comedy. It also challenges the images of Africa presented by British films and by novels, such as *Mister Johnson*. In that novel, Joyce Cary drew on his experiences as a district officer in Nigeria to present a vigorous portrait of a Nigerian *demi évolué* and a highly prejudiced image of Nigerian village life. In Lakunle, Soyinka created a stage character with such striking similarities to Johnson as to compel comparison. *The Lion and the Jewel* shows Soyinka challenging Cary's images of Africans and Africa point for point. He represents an African village full of creative vigour; a corrupt white surveyor, who is completely out-manoeuvred by a highly intelligent chief, Baroka – a man who justifies his policy of relative isolation for the village with conviction and insight. Soyinka's play directly confronts colonial and racial attitudes which are found in dozens of English novels, and which were particularly infuriating to a nationalist writer when found in the work of Joyce Cary, an accomplished novelist with first-hand experience of Nigeria who had compaigned energetically against the continuation of colonialism.

A Dance of the Forests was first presented in 1960, but it was, in part, a reworking of an earlier play and bears the marks of containing a creative response to the Western dramatic tradition.[4] *The Chorus of the Ants* was clearly inspired by an episode in the Kapek brothers' expressionist drama *The Insect Play*. The Triplets, equally clearly, are a variation on the vision of the future presented by the Triplets which Hecate summons up for Macbeth. The play's concern with the possibility of breaking out of a destructive cycle is a theme which has preoccupied European dramatists from Euripides to Shakespeare, J. B. Priestley and Jean-Paul Sartre. Indeed, throughout the play there are echoes and half-echoes of European writers and their works. Yet, with the possible exception of the Triplets, whose origin has been remarked by many, *A Dance* does not draw obtrusively on the European tradition: it impresses because it is firmly set in Soyinka's version of a Yoruba 'forest of a thousand daemons' or 'bush of ghosts'. Its cast-list includes Yoruba deities, and variations on them, and it incorporates Yoruba-style purification rituals and dance dramas within a structure which is derived from a New Year Festival. In its satire and thematic concerns, it addresses a community which was sometimes regarded as fatalistic, part of which was euphoric at the prospect of independence and part of which had become heady with nostalgia when contemplating Africa's past. While *A Dance of the Forests* drew inspiration from both European and Yoruba traditions, it was clearly addressed to a particular community at a particular point in history, a point at which change appeared to be possible.

After completing his BA at Leeds, Soyinka had begun a special study of the work of Eugene O'Neill as part of an MA. His choice of the American playwright, whose plays examine classical, historical, social and autobiographical themes, is in itself revealing: O'Neill's range and ambition impressed Soyinka. A comparison of the structure of an O'Neill play, *The Emperor Jones*, with Soyinka's play of the early sixties, *The Strong Breed*, is particularly rewarding. The pattern in both plays is of pursuit and flash-back within a context of ritual, and in both cases the protagonist's final encounter is in the nature of a vision. *The Strong Breed* benefits by employing the effective structure of O'Neill's play and by the challenge it contains to O'Neill's portrait of a black man and a black community. Soyinka handles ritual with far greater respect and insight than O'Neill, and his protagonist, though flawed, is far more complex than O'Neill's opportunist Emperor who verges on a racial stereotype.

After putting aside his MA work and moving to London, Soyinka came into contact with many of the most significant British playwrights and directors of the period. He also went to the cinema frequently and had some instruction in camera techniques. He was an angry young black man in a city responding to a cult of blackness in the arts, where an excited generation of African students awaited the Year of

Africa (1960) and where race riots in Notting Hill jolted a community which had complacently assumed it had no racial problems. Soyinka's intellectual attitudes were already formed: he attacked the complacent, both white and black; mourned the black victims of white racism, dismissed the patronising and sentimental, and scorned much that was being put on in the London theatre. Of the creative work he encountered at the Royal Court and elsewhere, he admired the invective of John Osborne; he approved of *The Kitchen* by Arnold Wesker (but not of Wesker's cultural attitudes); he enjoyed the use of popular traditions in Joan Littlewood's theatre of celebration; he respected the craftsmanship of some of the absurdists; he was enthusiastic about Peter Brook's productions which have often been characterised by an emphasis on ritual; he responded to the poetic-political theatre of John Arden whose *Serjeant Musgrave's Dance* was produced at the Court during 1959, and he wrote positively of the continuation of the Morality tradition in the theatre of Bertolt Brecht. He took part in an improvisation based on reports from Kenya, that is to say a Living Newspaper style production, and gained experience by directing first *The Swamp Dwellers* and then, with professionals, an evening of his own work which included a grim satirical piece which he has since tried to bury, *The Invention*.

On his return to Nigeria, Soyinka's activities in the theatre and his research into West African drama influenced his writing. Significantly, he completed *The Trials of Brother Jero* at the time when he was preparing to play Yang Sun in a production of Brecht's *Good Woman of Setzuan*. 'Significantly' because he borrows a technique used by Brecht in scene eight of *The Good Woman*, one which, in a sense, grows out of the story-telling tradition. *Camwood on the Leaves*, first broadcast in 1960, is in the

tradition of bourgeois tragedy pioneered by Frank Wede-
kind, but it is also an adventurous piece of radio drama
which makes original use of Yoruba folk-songs and it finds
the root of discord in the violation of African values. In the
radio comedy series *Broke-Time Bar*, Soyinka created a
group of vivid characters and involved them in plots
reminiscent of those encountered in popular comedy from
Commedia dell'arte to the Ghanaian Concert Party, a
tradition which Soyinka had encountered on a research trip
to Kumasi early in 1960. In *Night of the Hunted*, he
combined his fascination with expiatory rites with his
concern about the power of women. For his paper on *The
African Approach to Drama*, he drew on the accounts of
African festival theatre available in the library of University College, and on the ceremonies, rites, and rituals he had
watched. He rejected the romanticism and nostalgia with
which the Negritude school approached such manifesta-
tions and this opposition gave a critical edge to some of his
writing. Much of it, including *A Dance*, sounded an
invigoratingly abrasive and independent note with condemnation of literary ideologies.

In his work of the mid-sixties, Soyinka continued to draw
on the two traditions which he straddled. The revues were
particularly eclectic: they contained his versions, in Yoruba, of Yoruba folk-songs, and his adaptation of the English
song 'The Vicar of Bray'. One sketch combined an
indigenous sense of humour with a punch-line from a
Brecht poem and others were in the tradition of the Yoruba
comic theatre or the Leeds rag revues. The very title of
Before the Blackout recalled that of the best known, British
undergraduate revue of the early sixties, *Beyond the
Fringe*, a show which had introduced a new satirical
intensity into the London theatre. *Kongi's Harvest*, built
around a New Yam festival, owes much to the conventions

of African festival theatre and embodies a response to political developments in Nigeria and Africa during the first half of the 'Decade of Africa'. It also shows a kinship with *Serjeant Musgrave's Dance*, since both employ the technique of cross-cutting familiar from the cinema and are in the tradition of political theatre created by Brecht in *The Resistible Rise of Arturo Ui*. One specific debt is hinted at in the Organizing Secretary's reference to 'one uneasy crown which still eludes my willing head', a half-echo of a line from *Henry IV Part II*. In its use of contrasts and tableaux, its epic nature and its imposition of a pattern on the flow of history – but not in its political position – there are striking parallels between *Kongi's Harvest* and Shakespeare's chronicles. Indeed, the demands which Soyinka's shifting of scenes and 'open' conclusion make are of the same order as those made by Shakespeare.

In *The Road* the worlds of St Peter's Church and Abeokuta lorry-park come together and are given extra dimensions by *egungun* masquerades, a drivers' festival, Agemo celebrations and the Yoruba comic theatre tradition of slap-stick and satire. The European influences include the traditions of Aristophanes, the Theatre of the Absurd and the cinematic conventions of the flash-back and dissolve. The integration of traditions and conventions is particularly effective and the result is characteristic of Soyinka's theatre.

Two academic papers from the mid-sixties reflect Soyinka's thinking about the ritual origins of drama and the social responsibilities of playwrights. *The Fourth Stage* indicates parallels between Yoruba and classical Greek patterns of tragedy through a subjective analysis of an Ogun festival, and *The Role of the Writer in a Modern African State* concludes with an assessment and an assertion. 'The artist', Soyinka proclaimed, 'has always functioned in African society as the record of mores and experience of his society and as the voice of vision in his own time. It is time for him to respond to this essence of himself.' These lines, and these essays, show Soyinka's continuing concern to combine elements from Europe and Africa, and suggest that his position, while not totally unlike that of European writers, is rooted in African precedent and experience.

Madmen and Specialists was an act of exorcism, a self-purging of the bitterness and bile which had built up during the months in detention. Though there are moments at which Socratic dialogue, Absurdist humour and Swiftian satire are employed, these influences are firmly contained within a distinctive drama which was first presented to an international audience about an unnamed civil war and which has a generalized quality uncommon in Soyinka. Elements of Yoruba ritual, conventions of Yoruba word play, Yoruba songs and Yoruba attitudes give the play a 'local habitation'.

The plays of the early seventies were written out of confidence in the existence of African theatre: Soyinka had created such a distinctive theatre during the sixties that he was no longer worried about literary debt collectors hammering at his door. *Jero's Metamorphosis* draws its local qualities from the characters and humour it contains and the 'Roman circus' atmosphere which existed in Nigeria, but its structure is basically that of a situation comedy with a subversive sting in its tail. The European source of *The Bacchae* is obvious, but so too are the extensive and significant deviations from that source. The re-acquaintance with the classics and with the European tradition represented by the work on Euripides affected Soyinka's next, and most Shakespearean, play, *Death and the King's Horseman*. *Antony and Cleopatra* and, once again, Shakespeare's chronicle plays lie behind this study of suicide and of conflicting codes of honour. The form of the play makes it particularly accessible to audiences familiar with the European tradition, but its meaning challenges those audiences to come to terms with the Yoruba world-view, metaphysical system, religion and code of conduct. The nature of the challenge to European philosophy and attitudes to Africa in *Horseman* was extended in Soyinka's Cambridge lectures, published as *Myth, Literature and the African World*. The attitude shown by Simon Pilkings, the District Officer in *Horseman*, when confronted by the Yoruba sensibility is similar to that displayed by certain of the University administrators. The proper study of mankind may be man, but in the opinion of certain Cambridge authorities the proper place for a study by an African was the anthropology department.

While in Ghana during the seventies, Soyinka was attacked by those critics who argued for the 'decolonisation of African literature'. He replied to those who campaigned for simple diction and accessible images, who deplored what they termed 'Euro-modernist' complexity and who 'exposed' what they called 'The Scandalous Leeds-Ibadan Connection'. In spirited articles, Soyinka argued that language had to be fragmented and reassembled and that inherited local forms were subtle and complex – a point that has already emerged from this study.

Opera Wonyosi, produced in 1976, looked back to the earlier satirical revues and is the culmination of Soyinka's long-standing enthusiasm for Brecht's work. It contained attacks on various social anomalies, on tyranny and on national scandals from a leftist, but not a Marxist, position. When the production was criticised by radicals, Soyinka defended himself with an aggression which may have concealed a sense of injury, isolation and even betrayal. In the years which followed, he has continued, in the manner embarked on in *Opera*, to expose corruption in Nigerian society. He has done this in ways which show an increasingly firm grasp of the issues involved in writing for popular audiences. There is some evidence of the influence of the Living Newspaper tradition but the most prominent shaping forces are the political factors, the vast scale of the corruption and Soyinka's anxiety to communicate. Significantly, he used dialogue which incorporated pidgin, and musical idioms with a foot-tapping, hip-swinging, get-up-and-dance rhythm.

Requiem For a Futurologist is out of the mainstream of the work from this period. Apart from the spiritual and social environment which provoked and shaped it, a specific debt can be traced to the work of Jonathan Swift. In this instance Soyinka took a situation which had arisen following Swift's attack on almanac-maker John Partridge as a starting point for his play. Having decided to use the idea, he then explored it in the context of his society and dramatised it with intellectual vigour, resourceful wit and vivid characterisation. The episode proved capable of conveying a comment on the confusions and credulity of some Nigerians and created a situation which appealed to a local sense of humour.

Blues of a Prodigal, in 1984 was the proper outcome of Soyinka's well-documented interest in film, in writing for the cinema and in directing. Much of his work had creatively introduced cinematic conventions into the theatre, some of it even had the mark of a frustrated screen-writer. Indeed *The Road* had, apparently, been conceived as a film. With *Blues* he took up the challenge to use the resources of modern technology to communicate African experience and modes of perception.[5]

In some respects *A Play of Giants* is reassuringly familiar to those who have followed developments in the Western theatre during the last century – it was significantly premiered in New Haven. However, in its challenge to the audience it is uncompromisingly African. Soyinka is passionately concerned about what has been happening on the African continent and *A Play of Giants* presents this concern through a ferocious satirical onslaught on those who betray and foul the continent. Like the rocket–launcher which Kamini trains on the United Nations Building at the end of the play, the 'vehicle' Soyinka has chosen for his attack is 'made in there' – that is of non-African origin. But, of course, rocket–launchers have been used throughout the continent. There are Africans who fire them, Africans who have been bereaved by them, Africans who have been maimed by them. Soyinka seems to say 'we have taken foreign built rocket-launchers into our armouries, why should we not allow the writer the same liberty of choice of weapons?' The weapon he has chosen and suitably adapted is, in *A Play of Giants*, trained on those who Soyinka regards as enemies of Africa. It is fired with explosive results.

3
The Leeds Plays

At Leeds, Soyinka struggled with a tragedy about Apartheid. When he put it aside he wrote, at about the same time (1957–58) and with considerable ease, the two very different plays, *The Swamp Dwellers* and *The Lion and Jewel*, which opened doors for him in London and established his reputation in Nigeria. While *The Swamp Dwellers* bears the marks of its author's academic background and displays only a few features of his characteristic style, *The Lion and the Jewel* is assured and remarkable. It has been brought to life on stages across Africa and is established as one of Soyinka's most effective, provocative and amusing plays.

Soyinka started writing *The Swamp Dwellers* after reading that oil had been found in marketable quantities in the Niger Delta.[1] This news prompted him to think about other communities he knew which had experienced a similar access to sudden wealth and to ponder the impact of wealth on relationships in a hitherto subsistence economy. The setting he chose for the play is a hut raised on stilts above the swamps and even before the lights come up on the stage the audience is introduced to the environment in which the drama is set: there are sounds of *frogs, rain and other swamp noises*. The hut is constructed from *marsh stakes* and *hemp ropes* and in it Makuri makes baskets from rushes while his wife, Alu, works at her *adire* cloth. This image of a couple living at subsistence level and using raw materials from their immediate environment is broken by the object which stands in the middle of the room, a barber's swivel chair. Through the chair, Soyinka indicates that a different and distant world is making an impact on Makuri and Alu's home. In the course of the play, he suggests that the world from which swivel chairs are sent is a source of pain, disappointment and frustration; it is a place where greed dominates, where family relationships break down and where the hard-hearted prosper.

Soyinka tells the story of Makuri and Alu and their twin sons, Awuchike and Igwezu. Ten years before the play opens, Awuchike had set off across the swamps for the city to seek his fortune. Nothing has been heard of him since. Some months before the opening dialogue, Igwezu had planted his fields, provided the Kadiye, or priest of the Serpent of the Swamp, with a calf to sacrifice to the Serpent and left with his young wife for the city. There he found Awuchike alive and wealthy, but 'dead' to his parents and to any sense of family responsibility. Igwezu had struggled and had earned enough money to fulfil his promise to send his father a swivel chair. But he had not prospered, his wife had left him for his rich brother and he had been forced to use the harvest he anticipated from his fields as security on a loan from that same rich and unbrotherly brother. Very shortly before the lights come up on Makuri and Alu at the start of *The Swamp Dwellers*, Igwezu had returned home and had, almost immediately, rushed out to inspect his crops. A desolate sight awaited him for the rains had been very heavy and the crops have been ruined by floods: the Kadiye, who had promised protection in return for the sacrificial calf, had failed him and, indeed, the community. Far from being embarrassed or ashamed, the Kadiye, hearing that Igwezu has returned and anticipating that he has made his fortune in the city, visits Makuri's house and asks to be shaved by Igwezu. Eventually he seats himself in the swivel chair, thereby incautiously placing himself at the mercy of the disappointed young man. With a razor at the priest's throat and his hand quivering with rage and spiritual confusion, Igwezu pours out a stream of questions about the priest's promises and conduct. At one moment he seems sufficiently angry to slice into the rolls of fat beneath the priestly chin. But he restrains himself and he eventually allows the terrified Kadiye to scamper away. Then he faces up to his own position and flees, knowing that the villagers will demand his blood when they hear how he has humiliated their priest.

This resumé gives little idea of the devices which Soyinka employed in telling his story: the narrative emerges through a variety of exchanges and the audience must be attentive in order to piece it together. Soyinka wrote this play in prose, in a naturalistic style; the unities are adhered to and prejudices for the well-made play are not violated. But it moves on occasions towards the symbolist and melodramatic; it is a play of mood and atmosphere, constructed so as to provide the audience with ample opportunity to make comparisons and reach judgements. Indeed, Soyinka repeatedly makes his points through implied contrasts – a characteristic feature of much of his work. The most obvious contrast in *The Swamp Dwellers* is that between the twin brothers, who look alike but behave very differently. There is also a contrast between the women in the family: the text creates an opportunity to set the weakness and infidelity of Igwezu's wife against the strength and virtue of Alu, who had remained faithful to her husband despite temptations from visiting traders. Soyinka introduces one major character, a Blind Beggar, largely for the purpose of establishing contrasts and comparisons. We gather that after losing his crops to locusts, the Beggar had left his home in Bukanji and walked South, passing quickly through 'the city', searching for land to cultivate. He is 'tall and thin' and a Muslim, in most respects a striking contrast to the Kadiye. His experiences of misfortune provide a comparison with Igwezu's, and his determination to find satisfying employment creates a pattern of endeavour which, it is hinted, the young man may be able to follow.

In order to establish the contrasts and bring out the comparisons, Soyinka has introduced many, too many, exits and entrances; many, too many, arrivals and departures. In this instance the setting and the convention are at odds with the numerous juxtapositions he has arranged. In subsequent works he employed locations and evolved flexible conventions which enabled him to confront his audiences with a variety of characters and episodes and to invite them to make comparisons and contrasts without a sense of unease.

Though flawed by its unsuitable form, *The Swamp Dwellers* should not be dismissed entirely. The revelations about experiences and disappointments make an emotional impact. The symbol of the city as a place where fortunes are made and where, as in the treacherous swamps, sons may 'die' is established with subtlety and is convincing. The language is, for the most part, crisp and evocative, with occasional and effective use of proverbs, particularly by Makuri. Sometimes the dialogue contains hints of the powerful vehicle of dramatic expression which Soyinka was to fashion out of contemporary, Nigerian English, as when Igwezu says: 'The city reared itself in the air, and with the strength of its legs of brass kicked the adventurer in the small of his back.' Sometimes, in the references to 'pottage' and 'slough' for instance, the registers of the Bible and *Pilgrim's Progress* are distractingly present, but such lapses are rare.

The Swamp Dwellers was first presented by a group of young people in London, with Soyinka as Igwezu, during 1958. The following year it was produced by Geoffrey Axworthy at University College, Ibadan, with Christine Clinton and Dapo Adelugba in the cast. Critics then, and since, have been divided in their reactions to Igwezu and the Kadiye, their ideas about the meaning of the play and their responses to the ending. Igwezu has been seen as a portrait of the playwright and as a sentimental hero. The Kadiye has been regarded as a grotesque villain by some and as refreshingly resourceful by others. The play, as a whole, has been praised as an evocative study in disappointment and condemned for not preaching a positive message by showing the villagers casting off their superstitions and marching off to construct dykes and increase the amount of land available for farming.[2] At moments the play certainly becomes sentimental and melodramatic. It is an early work and one in which the intensity of Soyinka's feelings, his identification with Igwezu and his scorn for the Kadiye, could find no suitable outlet within the genre he had chosen. His purpose in writing the play would not, however, have been served by an ending which suggested that a land-reclamation scheme would solve all problems. Rather, he was seeking, through a response to a news item about oil finds, for an image which would convey his concern about the social changes brought about by access to wealth. Easy money, whatever its source, destroys, as the experience of the oil-boom years in Nigeria showed only too clearly.

What Soyinka wished to convey by his ending to *The Swamp Dwellers* is not absolutely clear: it is an ambiguous coda. After the Beggar's question/statement: 'But you will return, master?' Igwezu walks slowly off. The Beggar's final speech, a monologue of sorts, is obscure, but nevertheless establishes a distinctive mood. Together with the stage image which accompanies it – the Beggar stands still as the light fades on him – the lines suggest that Igwezu will return. The Beggar says:

> The swallows find their nest again when the cold is over. Even the bats desert dark holes in the trees and flap wet leaves with wings of leather. There were wings everywhere as I wiped my feet against your threshold. I heard the cricket scratch himself beneath the armpit as the old man said to me . . . I shall be here to give account.
>
> (*Collected Plays, I*, hereafter *C.P., I*, p.112.)

The swallows provide a pattern which the young man may follow, but what precisely the bats or the cricket represent is not clear. The density of the imagery means that the words, which defy elucidation in the study, pass for little on the stage; there the gestures and the final tableau are all important. The Beggar's blessing counts for more than the cricket's scratching, and his stillness and solidity are deeply impressive: he becomes – almost – a statue. The oil-lamps go out slowly and the moonlight falls on the unmoving figure who has joined the barber's swivel chair as a strange presence in Makuri's room, an encouraging presence, a man of integrity, a figure who embodies some hope for the future.

The endings of Soyinka's plays almost always pose

problems. They do not provide resolutions or finales so much as 'new beginnings' or moments of temporary quiet after acts of violence or explosions of emotional tension. In his final tableaux there are configurations of forces and presences which reflect the state of flux which exists in the stage-world. Handled carefully by performers, lighting designers, musicians and directors these 'pauses' – or processions to new encounters – can be satisfying in the theatre. They provide as final an image as the audience is entitled to expect. Soyinka shows an awareness in *The Swamp Dwellers*, as in later and more complex plays, of life and history moving almost in cycles. The image of the Mobius Strip, which he employs in his poem 'Idanre', is useful: in a sense a cycle or revolution is complete, yet the final situation is not identical to that at the beginning of the play. We have completed a circuit of the Mobius Strip.

The Lion and the Jewel was 'triggered' by reading, several years after the event took place, about Charlie Chaplin's marriage at the age of nearly sixty to the teenaged Oona O'Neill. From Chaplin's marriage, Soyinka's mind moved on to consider the marriages contracted by senior men in his society to very young women. Sandalled octogenerian chiefs, *obas* and *bales* had married teenagers despite challenges from school teachers in canvas shoes. Soyinka's play celebrates the vigour, cunning and energy of such elders, and their ability both to survive and to satisfy their appetites in maturity for the fresh and youthful. In and through Lakunle, the playwright attacks those in canvas shoes, the half-baked and half-educated, who have little awareness of their own community and only a very superficial knowledge of Europe – from which continent they are nevertheless intent on importing such frivolous activities as cocktail parties and beauty competitions.

This play is set in Ilujinle, a relatively remote village, which, under the guidance of its *bale*, Baroka, has re-

mained largely isolated. Some decades before the play is
set, Baroka managed to have the railway line diverted so
that it did not pass near to the village and, though he has
made some concessions to change – there is a school in the
village and his palace staff have formed a union – Baroka is
still firmly in control. Shortly before the play begins,
Ilujinle has been visited by a photographer who has taken
pictures of the village, its chief and, particularly, of Sidi, a
very pretty young woman, the jewel of Ilujinle and of the
title of the play. In the opening sequence Sidi is courted by
Lakunle the village school-master, but, when the photographer arrives with copies of the magazine featuring Sidi,
Bale Baroka decides that he and no one else will possess
'the jewel of Ilujinle'. Through his eldest wife, Sadiku, the
Bale invites Sidi to dinner. When she refuses the invitation
and makes a disparaging comment about the Bale's age, he
sets another, more devious, plan in motion: he lies to
Sadiku that he has become impotent, knowing that she will
pass on this news and anticipating that Sidi's cheekiness will
draw her to his bedroom – the lion's den. The plan works
and, once he has a chance to talk to Sidi alone, he woos her
so subtly and plays on her vanity so effectively that he is
able to seduce her. When Lakunle hears what has happened, he declares that he is still prepared to marry Sidi,
but she will have nothing to do with him. She has, she says,
'felt the strength/The perpetual youthful zest/Of the panth-
er of the trees' and is happy to marry the sixty-two year old
chief. The play ends with Sadiku, 'the mother of brides',
invoking the fertile gods and Lakunle clearing a space
among the dancers for a new 'madonna'.

The settings are carefully chosen. *The Lion and the Jewel*
opens in '*A clearing on the edge of the market, dominated by
an immense odan tree. It is the village centre. The wall of the
bush school flanks the stage on the right . . .*' This setting

locates the play at the heart of the community: between the busy world of the traders and the class-room through which influences will seep into the society, and under a tree known for the depth and generosity of its shade.

With characteristic awareness of the impact of sound-effects, Soyinka indicates that a *chant of the 'Arithmatic Times'* issues from the school-room as the audience takes in the set. When Sidi enters she appears to be an unaffected village girl: her hair is plaited, she wears a locally-made wrapper and she carries a bucket of water on her head *with accustomed ease*. Lakunle, who sees her through the school-room window and accosts her a few moments later, is dressed so as to reveal his aspirations to sophistication in an English suit, but it is too small for him and in a style which has passed out of fashion. This picture of sartorial inelegance is completed by the inevitable canvas shoes. Throughout the play, Soyinka's strong aural and visual senses inform and comment on characters and events.

Soyinka has constructed his play with skill so as to intrigue and entertain his audience; he provides variety and establishes contrasts of characters and moods. In a pattern found in several of his works, *The Lion and the Jewel* opens with a lengthy dialogue, in this case an exchange in which Lakunle attempts to advance his suit with Sidi. He is interrupted by the news that the photographer has brought the magazines and by the extended dance drama sequence which follows this announcement. In the dance-drama the previous visit of the photographer is re-enacted.

The opening scene of the second part, *Noon*, moves Baroka's plot forward, but then shifts into the past with an account, in words and actions, of how Baroka bribed the Surveyor from the Public Works Department to divert the railway line, *The Mime of the White Surveyor*. After this bold flash-back, the play moves to Baroka's bedroom to show the self-indulgent chief having hairs plucked from his arm-pit and initiating his second plan.

Night starts with Sadiku's dance of triumph, moves on to the scene in which Sidi is seduced and then shifts back to the village centre for Lakunle's vigil. When news breaks of the forthcoming marriage, Lakunle is, briefly, bewildered and the community gathers to celebrate in a time-honoured style.

The convention which Soyinka devised is expressive and effective. It enables him to communicate all the exposition about the photographer's first visit in a dance-drama, a sequence which also gives Lakunle an opportunity to establish himself as a performer, provides Baroka with a chance to make an effective entrance and gives a lift to the play when it is in danger of getting 'too wordy'. These dance-dramas are 'plays within a play', but the sequence which concerns the past, *The Mime of the White Surveyor*, cannot be explained in terms of a community which simply enjoys performing. Soyinka need not have introduced this passage, yet it seems particularly suitable that he did so in view of the way in which African leaders had been presented by British novelists, Joyce Cary among them, and in order to provide an historical dimension to the portrait of Baroka.

The convention allowed Soyinka to compare and contrast Lakunle with Baroka. Although superficially very different in social standing and accomplishments, there are substantial similarities. Both are, for example, performers and sensualists, and both woo Sidi. Both also have ideas – very different ideas – about the future of Ilujinle: Baroka's policy is highly selective; Lakunle, on the other hand, is in favour of the wholesale adoption of the gaudy trimmings of Western material culture. Where Baroka has had a stamp-making machine constructed and hopes to levy a tax on 'the habit of talking with paper', Lakunle looks forward to an Ilujinle with a crowded social calendar, with the beauty competitions and cocktail parties attended by ladies in high-heeled shoes, with 'red paint' on their lips and their 'hair stretched like a magazine photo'.

The contrast between the two men in regard to role-playing and the use of language is presented with particular subtlety. In *Morning* the gauche Lakunle has to be bullied into taking part in the *Dance of the Lost Photographer*, once involved he performs with grace and reveals a mischievous sense of humour. Baroka, however, needs no begging, he is ready 'on cue' and plays his part with the relish of an experienced, indeed an habitual, actor. Both men enjoy using language. Lakunle has a knowledge of local idioms which he can employ with wit and effect, for instance, he picks up Sidi's 'have you no shame?' and aptly points out that 'That's what the stewpot said to the fire . . . But she was tickled just the same'. However, the school-teacher frequently lapses into barren, borrowed and bombastic rhetoric. His memory is cluttered with alien images and with quotations from romantic fiction and the Christian liturgy. He pleads: 'Sidi, my heart/Bursts into flowers with my love./ But you, you and the dead of this village/Trample it with feet of ignorance.' He swears he will 'Stand against earth, heaven and the nine/Hells.' He quotes: 'And the man shall take the woman/And the two shall be together/As one flesh.' In an enjoyable passage in the opening dialogue with Sidi, he condemns the payment of bride-price with a list of fine-sounding words which he has learnt from his *Shorter Companion Dictionary*. When he runs out of appropriate adjectives, he calls into service others of doubtful suitability and eventually splutters to a halt. At this point Sidi asks, in an image which sums up her response to Lakunle's use of language, 'Is the bag empty?'

Baroka's attitude to language is entirely different from Lakunle's: he handles words with care, delighting in their individual qualities. His manipulation of sense, image and sound is well illustrated in the seduction scene, where he speaks, for example, of progress 'Which makes all roofs and faces look the same.' He evokes an image of 'Virgin plots of lives, rich decay/And the tang of vapour rising from/Forgotten heaps of compost, lying/Undisturbed . . .' In these lines the very stench of decay is presented in positive terms for the decaying vegetation of today will, it is recognised, promote growth tomorrow. Baroka, the image reveals, is a conservationist ahead of his time, who regards isolation as part of a plan for the future. The image of Ilujinle as a compost heap is one which reverberates, indeed it draws attention to a concept which recurs again and again in Soyinka's work and which has become a feature of his view of life. This is summed up in a line from 'Requiem': 'Rust is ripeness', which suggests that in evidence of decay is to be found maturity and fruitfulness.

There are occasions in *The Lion and the Jewel* when the dialogue and speech-making are over-extended. As a young playwright, Soyinka depended too much on speeches, but he showed even in his early work that he was aware of the value of gesture, dance and mime as means of communication. The sequences of physical action are strategically placed in this play so as to provide comments and establish rhythms. Some of them are particularly revealing and some are highly stylised. For instance, when Sidi enters the Bale's bedroom she finds him engaged in a trial of strength with a wrestler and embarks on an exchange of proverbs which complements the wrestling match. When Baroka throws his adversary, he performs an action which anticipates his final conquest of Sidi – an embrace which is not shown. As Sidi's head falls on the

Bale's shoulder, the lights dim and dancers burst on to the stage. These performers, who cross and re-cross the stage and then reappear in the market-clearing, dance Baroka's story, or a version of it. The performance consists of a number of women pursuing a masked, male-figure, 'Baroka'; 'Baroka' performs a dance of virility but eventually wearies and is no longer capable of responding to the tantalising motions of the women; Sadiku then enters the dance to 'join in at the kill.' This sequence is highly stylised, deeply influenced by Yoruba conventions and, since Baroka is even at that moment enjoying Sidi, deeply ironic.

The marriage dance which brings the play to an end, but which cannot be adquately described as a 'grand finale' or 'closing number', is particularly important in establishing the final mood of the play. It follows the invocation of the 'fertile gods', the blessing of the bride, and a song which anticipates a rapturous fecundity. The stage directions indicate that a *festival air* is *fully pervasive* as Sidi leads the celebrants in song and Lakunle, showing no ill-effects after losing Sidi, clears a space in the crowd. This is not a conclusion in the conventional sense, but a moment of transition, a pause before a 'new beginning': Sidi is moving into a new role and Lakunle embarking on a new relationship. In the final sequence, Soyinka seems to say: 'Respond to the music and the dancing: float on the mood established by the oil-lamps, by Sidi's joy and by Lakunle's resilience. We are back in the clearing where we began, a day has passed and matters no longer stand quite where they did. Take away this image and think about it.'

The first production of *The Lion and the Jewel* was greeted by criticism of some of the details of the text. Reviewers found fault with Sadiku's name, which, it was argued, was inappropriate for a woman; with Sidi's manner of addressing the Bale, which was considered 'disrespectful', and with Baroka's 'European-style trick' of inviting Sidi to supper: 'a Bale needs no subterfuge of this kind', it was objected, 'he can simply command'.[3] These are minor points and not ones which Soyinka has found it necessary to address himself to in published editions of the text. The first reviewers, together with those critics who considered the play lewd, failed to recognise that it was in a unique convention: a satirical musical comedy, which used carica- ture, exaggeration and simplification to provoke a response and stir up discussion about the forces present in the country at the time.

Subsequent critical discussion of the play has frequently been based on the assumption that Baroka represents static, 'traditional' African values, that Lakunle represents western civilisation, and that Soyinka, in a reactionary mood, favoured Baroka by letting him win the girl, Sidi, who 'represents' the new generation. This assessment is based on several mis-readings. Baroka is a *bale,* he holds a position of influence in Yoruba society, but this is not a static community. The 'tradition' in which he exists is constantly changing; *bales* have to be politically agile, they have to come to terms with new developments and anticipate change. Baroka is highly intelligent and a 'survivor'; he has listened to what the Christians' Holy Book says; he has let the palace workers form a union, and he has got his blacksmiths to make a printing press. He is, in his own way, responding to the winds of change which are blowing by trimming his sails. Lakunle, on the other hand, far from representing western civilisation, has no claim to be a representative of anything other than *demi évolués* with missionary prejudices; he is infatuated with the vulgar and tawdry in English life – blown off his feet. Sidi is young, attractive, independent, and disrespectful. Despite her plaits and wrapper, she is at odds with the role often ascribed to young Yoruba women.

Those who find a bland, reactionary message in this play have misread or mis-watched it: *The Lion and the Jewel* is a celebration of Baroka, his vitality and cunning, and it recommends a syncretistic approach. A key statement of the playwright's vision is found in the seduction scene where Baroka argues that 'the old must flow into the new'. This argument pervades the form as well as the meaning of the play, for *The Lion and the Jewel* stands at the confluence of two traditions: the Yoruba masque and the European satirical musical. It is an early masterpiece, capable of unleashing tremendous power on the stage, of provoking and entertaining, of speaking to those familiar with either the Yoruba or the European tradition, and of challenging them to respond to a new theatrical experience.

4
The Independence Plays

During 1960, the year of Soyinka's return home and of Nigeria's independence, three of the published canon of Soyinka's plays were first produced. While clearly part of the same sensibility which had created *The Swamp Dwellers* and *The Lion and the Jewel*, these plays reflected developments in Nigerian affairs and the remoteness of the possibility for change in that country. The indications can be seen in suspicions concerning the quality of the leaders who were settling into positions of power, in the challenge posed to the glib optimism of many of the population and in the determination to draw more deeply on African traditions.

The Trials of Brother Jero (1960) was written, according to Dapo Adelugba, over a week-end in response to a request from the Students' Dramatic Society for a one-act drama which could be performed as part of a triple-bill.[1] Since the Arts Theatre at University College, Ibadan, was undergoing alterations, the play had to be suitable for production in the dining-room of one of the halls of residence, on an improvised stage and with a minimum of lighting resources. In writing, in some respects, *The Trials* 'to order' Soyinka drew on his experience of separatist sects in Abeokuta, Lagos and Ibadan, and on the knowledge, gained partly through observation of his mother, of Yoruba women traders. He was aware, as he worked out the story-line, of the influence wielded by the prophets, or praying church leaders, over powerful members of the community, including members of parliament. He knew that as independence approached, the influence of the 'prophets' would be crucial.

The Trials tells the story of Brother Jeroboam, 'a prophet by birth and by inclination', who, after serving his apprenticeship, has out-manoeuvred his mentor and established his own rights to territory on Victoria Beach. The Old Prophet had cursed Jero 'with the curse of the Daughters of Discord', and it is, appropriately, women who pose the greatest threat to Jero's continued prosperity. When the play opens, Jero owes a cloth trader, Amope, £1.8.9 for a velvet cape, and we see the determined debt collector laying siege to the hut in Ajete where he sleeps. It so happens that Amope's husband, a Chief Messenger called Chume, is one of Jero's most fervent followers, but, at the start of the play, as at the start of many comedies, the characters are unaware how extensively their lives are intertwined. Jero avoids paying his debt, conducts morning worship on the beach, and is distracted by a passing 'daughter of discord'. Chume, we gather, wants Jero's permission to beat his wife, but the prophet, unaware of course that Chume's wife is the 'vulture crouched on (his) bed-post', and realising that Chume must be kept discontented if he is to remain in the congregation, refuses to grant him dispensation. When Jero leaves his congregation in pursuit of a young woman, Chume conducts the worship to an ecstatic pitch. From the conversation which follows his return, Jero is able to work out that Chume is Amope's husband and, with some relief, gives him permission to thrash her. The plan for revenge backfires, however, because Amope reveals to Chume that the man who owes her money – and sleeps at Ajete – is none other than Brother Jero! Chume's eyes are opened: he realises that Jero sleeps in a hut and not, as he had believed, in sanctifying discomfort on the beach, and he sets off intent on murdering the perfidious prophet. He comes upon him ensnaring a Member of Parliament in his web of honeyed promises and puts him to flight. Even Jero's departure before Chume's cutlass works to the charlatan's advantage, for the MP thinks the prophet has literally vanished from his sight. Jero escapes from Chume's wrath and summons the police to arrest the gullible Chief Messenger. In an address to the audience, the prophet indicates that he will, with the MP's help, have Chume confined to a lunatic asylum. The play draws to an end with the MP clearly within Jero's power: in a final tableau, the politician prostrates himself before the 'prophet', crying 'Master' – the triumph of the deceiver is complete.

At the beginning of the play, Jero introduces himself to the audience with the words 'I am a Prophet'. Direct address of this particular sort is a technique which Soyinka had not used before and has not used since. When a little later Jero says 'my whole purpose in coming here is to show you one rather eventful day in my life' it appears that Soyinka is finding common ground between a convention used by Brecht in *The Good Woman of Setzuan* and the flourishing story-telling tradition of the Yorubas. The technique allows him to establish Jero's character, create rapport with the audience and fill in essential background.

In order to prevent the monologue becoming boring, and because Soyinka rarely tells his audience about an episode when he can *show* it to them, he brings the Old Prophet, hurling his curses at Jero's head, out of the past and onto the stage. The 'Brechtian' technique is useful and Soyinka employs it to good effect.

With the spectacular entrance of Chume and Amope on a bicycle, the play gathers pace. The couple, who come to an awkward halt in the middle of the stage, are vibrantly alive; in their relationship and dialogue Soyinka strikes notes which many have recognised as familiar. Amope is aggressive and assured, full of complaints about her husband; she is also practical and determined, equipped to besiege Jero. Chume is, almost inevitably, repressed, resentful, long-suffering, and much put upon, but he is not lacking in spirit. After his first exit, the play begins to move subtly in two directions – one farcical, as Jero attempts to escape through the window of the hut and Amope, without looking back, says, 'Where do you think you are going?'; the other rooted in the every-day exchanges of Yoruba markets: greetings, business transactions, insults, often highly imaginative insults.

In the worship of Jero's congregation, Soyinka finds opportunity to bring onto the stage the rhythmic chanting and the apparently total involvement which is a feature of African pentecostal churches. It is an exciting stage spectacle, but it is not *mere* spectacle. Chume's participation is particularly intense and revealing, and in the course of it the audience becomes aware how much Chume's domestic and professional frustrations find outlets in his religion. First when he prays ('If I could only beat her once, only once',) and then, in a masterfully orchestrated sequence, when, leading the congregation in prayer, his intercessions merge with imperatives ('I say those who dey walka today, give them own bicycle tomorrow. Those who have bicycle today, they will ride their own car tomorrow.') This sequence, which few who see it well performed can forget, leads into a neatly constructed encounter in which Chume, emboldened by Jero, confronts his formidable spouse. The exchange is followed in turn by the final scene, containing some well-directed political satire at the expense of Members of Parliament.

The play is a successful combination of farce, characterised by slapstick, concealed identities and neat coincidences, with brillantly observed and sharply realised details of Yoruba life, and with well-directed satire. The vitality of the piece is partly the result of the appeal and personality of Brother Jero, who, from his very first speech, establishes a special relationship with audiences. Though he is a villain, a hypocrite, a liar and a cheat his disconcerting honesty has won him friends on every stage he has stepped on to. Part of his attraction lies in his eloquence; he can, for example, adopt an ornate, ecclesiastical register, full of high-minded statements, rhetorical flourishes and visionary insights. To the MP, he recalls a vision – in lines which have won Soyinka himself the title of 'Prophet' –

> I saw this country plunged into strife.
> I saw the mustering of men, gathered in
> the name of peace through strength.
> And at a desk, in a large gilt room,
> great men of the land awaited your
> decision. (*C.P. II*, p.169)

The audience delights in knowing that this is only the public side of 'the articulate hero of Christ's crusade', that the apostate has a weakness for women and that he often emerges from encounters with them with his face scratched and his clothes torn. Such is the vigorous theatricality of this character that Soyinka wisely resurrected him fifteen years later, fifteen years in which Jero had become the most popular theatrical character in English-speaking Africa.

After the first production of *The Trials* several undergraduates at Ibadan expressed their outrage at what they considered Soyinka's attack on Christianity. Since then the play has been assessed more calmly, and the targets of the satire have been correctly identified as the hypocrisy of some of those who aspire to lead and the gullibility of those who allow themselves to be lead astray. More generally, the play indicates the spiritual confusion and, by extension, the political naïveté of many of the playwright's fellow countrymen and fellow human beings.

Criticism has often been directed against the ending: it has, for instance, been described as abrupt and inconclusive. Given the nature of the occasion for which this play was written, the ending is perfectly valid. It is true that a bleak and sinister mood is created in the final scene, but that is entirely appropriate. Soyinka was writing for a nation which was about to become independent, and about whose future and future leaders he was deeply concerned. His satirical instincts, already highly developed, identified an easy target and he loosed a wounding shaft. As it struck home, he called for that ending which often follows a punch–line and concludes a revue sketch; the quick black–out. All productions I have seen have been followed by delighted applause.

Camwood on the Leaves, premiered only a few months after Jero, is concerned with stages of growth and concepts of tragedy. Sub-titled 'a rite of childhood passage', *Camwood* was first broadcast, very appropriately, as part of the independence celebrations. It is set in a Yoruba community in which Christian teaching has made some impact, and particularly concerns Isola, the son of the Reverend Erinjobi and his wife, Moji. Isola has repeatedly disobeyed his father and he has made Morunke Olumorin, the daughter of a powerful local couple, pregnant. The play takes place during the night following the revelation of Morunke's pregnancy and after Isola has refused to endure his punishment, a beating from his father, 'like a man'. Isola has run away with Morunke to a shelter outside the town, where he sleeps fitfully and dreams. It transpires that he keeps a gun in the shelter in the hope of killing a 'boa' (Soyinka uses this word for a python) which lives nearby and threatens the life of a tortoise and her young. Isola has projected his feelings about his parents onto these creatures; he calls the boa 'Erinjobi' and the tortoise 'Moji'. When the last shot in the gun is accidentally fired, Isola, followed by Morunke, returns to the town, breaks into his father's study and steals ammunition. The alarm is sounded, the community aroused and a chase begins. Cornered in some bushes and joined by Morunke, Isola fires at and kills his approaching father, believing, it seems, that he is aiming at the boa.

Though this is the only published radio-play from Soyinka's hand, it was not his first or his last. Indeed, he had written plays for radio some nine years previously and he had a great amount of broadcasting experience to draw on when considering how best to employ the medium of radio to create African radio drama. Each of his plays had been innovative in one way or another, *Camwood* made particularly effective use of sounds, songs and the juxtaposition of events. His particular concerns in this play were to bring the past into the experience of the play and to provide a social and emotional context in which a tragedy of adolescence could be played out. His solution to the first problem – the use of dream sequences – was not original, but it made good use of radio as a medium and the technique was handled with skill. In the shelter by the mangrove swamp, Isola is tormented by nightmares in which his confrontations with his father pass before his eyes – and enter the ears of the listeners. Having established the youth's waywardness and defiance in the past, Soyinka builds up expectations of his downfall. The playwright carefully prepares for what would otherwise be the melodrama of the closing moments of the play.

Radio and the cinema are particularly suitable media for those writers, like Soyinka, who work through contrasts to create emotional effects and to prod the audience into making judgments. In *Camwood* there are rapid and significant juxtapositions of scenes, montage effects created by moving from the parsonage to the forest path, then to the hut and back again to the parsonage. Through sound effects and clues in the dialogue, Soyinka locates his scenes quickly and establishes contrasts effectively.

Between the scenes, to provide links and create a social and emotional context, he makes extensive use of folksongs. The songs establish moods, evoke a world-view and bring home, once again, the musical dimension of Soyinka's culture, talent and theatre. In an interview, the playwright described *Camwood* as 'the aural equivalent of an *egungun* masquerade', and, although the full significance of this comparison remains to be explored, the songs are clearly an essential part of Soyinka's attempt to root his play in an existing performance tradition.

Camwood on the Leaves is a brilliantly constructed and deeply moving drama, which invites contrast with the European tradition of adolescent tragedy. In that tradition the pregnancy of a young girl is often at the root of the suffering and the audience's sympathy is usually drawn to support rebellious youth in its conflict with crabbed age. In

Camwood, however, Morunke's pregnancy causes no undue consternation, it is revealingly described as 'a child's mistake'. The root of this Yoruba tragedy is located in a young man's *hubris*, in Isola's disrespectful attitude to the Reverend Erinjobi, most blatantly apparent in his refusal to take a beating from his father. The play, like most tragedies, establishes a sense of inevitability about the eventual shooting of Erinjobi, an action anticipated by – and finally merged with – Isola's plans to kill the (sacred) python. All societies abhor parricide, but the Yoruba, to whom respect for old men is very important, regard it as particularly heinous: Isola, the parricide, is destined to go through life as an outcast. *Camwood* is the first of several Soyinka plays to have a violent finale, and is unique in having no 'epilogue' to suggest the impact of that violence. It relies on the dirge, 'Agbe' which wells up and which, since it has been heard earlier, completes a cycle. The words are the same, but clearly much has changed since 'Agbe' was first heard.

By laying bare a Yoruba tragedy constructed on characteristically Yoruba attitudes to pregnancy, pythons, punishments and parents, Soyinka was contributing to the self-apprehension of his people on the eve of independence. At a period of transition from colonialism, it was appropriate that he should provide a 'rite of passage' which implied a contrast between his society and the cultural traditions of the imperial power which had ruled it, which had endeavoured to impose values on it, and which had often denied the claim of Africans to such concepts as tragedy.

Camwood is a play to which Soyinka has returned, first to ensure belatedly its publication and, more recently, to stage and video it. These actions suggest the importance which he attaches to this too often neglected masterpiece.

Through *Camwood*, he established himself in the field of radio drama and marked the coming of age of a nation; from it he moved on to a more ambitious but, if a comparison of essentially 'unlike' works is made, a less successful undertaking.

It has been claimed that *A Dance of the Forests* was 'commissioned' for the celebration of Nigerian independence. This is not true, a significant portion of the text was taken over from an earlier work *The Dance of the African Forest*, an anti-Apartheid play. The following comment from the playwright clearly locates the play in a general context: '*A Dance of the Forests* was not a play about the Nigerian situation; it was a general thing. The independence celebration in 1960 was just an appropriate occasion to p-resent it.[2] In giving reasons why it was appropriate he said later 'after Independence some of those new rulers were going to behave exactly like their forebears did, just exploit the people.' He was, he continued, interested in 'taking another look at that history and saying: "The euphoria should be tempered by the reality of the eternal history of oppression".' A major theme in the play concerns the possibility of making a break with the past, of a new beginning, but there is much, too much, else.

With *A Dance*, Soyinka's drama becomes considerably more ambitious and obscure. In trying to come to terms with the structure and vision of this difficult play, the reader discovers that the narrative line is only one of several aspects which make an impresion. An unnamed community has held discussions as to how best to celebrate a festival, *The Gathering of the Tribes*, and before *A Dance* starts certain preparations have been made. Demoke, a carver, has transformed a giant silk-cotton tree into a totem; Adenebi, the Council Orator, has arranged for representatives from among the illustrious dead to be invited; the scattered sons and daughters of the soil, the beautiful but hard-hearted Rola amongst them, have been summoned home to join in the celebration. Events do not fall out as expected: while working on the totem, Demoke had come to resent his apprentice, Oremole, who was able to climb higher than he could; in a fit of jealousy he sent the assistant tumbling to his death and then lopped off the top of the tree, thereby offending Eshuoro, (a deity Soyinka created out of the fusion of Eshu the God of Fate and the cult of Oro.) Now that the totem is complete, the area around it has been cleared and Demoke no longer recognises it.

Soyinka provides a preamble to the play, a testimony from Aroni the one-legged one, which indicates the pattern that is followed when the 'dance' starts. This statement introduces the groups involved in the drama: the dead, the living, and the deities, both major and minor. The dead who arrive are remarkable, a man and a woman who have shown great courage and endured great suffering, but they are not the glamorous, gorgeously dressed, tyrannical rulers of a vanished African kingdom for whom Adenebi had hoped. The Dead Man had been castrated for his principles and the Dead Woman is pregnant with the Half-Child, whom she has carried through many generations. In the course of the play we are encouraged to focus our attention on three of the living; Adenebi, Rola and Demoke, whose murder of Oremole has, it seems, closed the final link in a chain or, to use another image, completed a circle. The dance can proceed. The three human beings are brought together, and, under the guidance of a major deity, Forest Head, conducted deep into the forest, the setting for many Yoruba adventure stories, for initiation rites and for the meetings of secret cults. After revealing exchanges and the intervention of various gods, particularly the vindictive and aggrieved Eshuoro and Ogun, who protects Demoke, the three humans are taken back to previous existences in the Court of Mata Kharibu. In a flash back, *The Welcome of the Dead*, we see them commit crimes similar to those they have been responsible for as 'living characters'.

A Dance of the Forests continues with an extended rite which incorporates *The Chorus of the Spirits, The Chorus of the Ants, The Masque of the Triplets* and *The Dance of the Half-Child*. Demoke bravely intervenes in this last dance and catches hold of the Half-Child; when he attempts to restore it to its mother, the Dead Woman, Eshuoro blocks his way and appeals to Forest Head, who says (*more to himself*):

> Trouble me no further. The fooleries of beings whom I have fashioned closer to me weary and distress me. Yet I must persist, knowing that nothing is ever altered. My secret is my eternal burden – to pierce the encrustations of soul-deadening habit, and bare the mirror of original nakedness – knowing full well, it is all futility. (*C.P.1*, p.71)

Demoke is told that the Half-Child is a 'doomed thing' but, after a moment's hesitation, he entrusts the child to its mother, the Dead Woman – who seems to want it despite the curse which it carries. Aroni leads the mother and the child away. Forest Head withdraws, and Eshuoro, with a *loud yell of triumph*, rushes off accompanied by his supporter. These somewhat bewildering events are followed by *The Dance of the Unwilling Sacrifice* in which Demoke is compelled by Eshuoro and his jester to bear a sacrificial basket to the top of the carved totem. As Demoke climbs, Eshuoro sets fire to the base of the totem;

the carver falls; Ogun catches him, carries him to the front of the stage and reunites him with the villagers who have been searching the forest. The effects of 'the dance' are then elliptically examined and the play draws to an end. This account reflects what happens in the version printed in *Collected Plays 1*, but there are at least four endings in existence, evidence of some uncertainty on Soyinka's part and of the difficulties he encountered in staging the conclusion.[3]

From this summary it is apparent that *A Dance* is much more complicated than anything encountered this far. While employing an innovative convention and carrying on a vigorous dialogue with the Western theatre, the play's deepest inspiration is defiantly and deliberately African. It is constructed on the pattern of a New Year Festival and, at various points, draws on traditions of African dance and on African rituals.

The language shows the varied influences at work in the play. The dramatic styles include the staccatto Beckettian opening exchanges, such as:

Dead woman: This is the place
Dead man: . . . Unless of course I came up too soon. It is such a long time and such a long way.
Dead woman: No one to meet me. I know this is the place. (*C.P.1*, p.7.)

There are also the proverb-filled utterances of the village elder, Agboreko, ('proverbs to bones and silence'); the bureaucratic statements of Adenebi ('We perform all the formalities'); the guilt-ridden, philosophical confession of Demoke, who describes himself as 'a slave to heights'; the taunts of the aggressive Rola ('He'll die in his bed but he'll die alone'); the invocation of the Dirge-man, ('Leave the dead/Some room to dance'); the imaginative insults of Murete ('You . . . mucus off a crab's carbuncle. You steam of fig pus from the duct of a stumbling bat.'); the threats of Oro whose 'voice is no child's lullaby to human ears'; and the Crier's formal addresses ('To all such as dwell in these Forests; Rocks devils/Earth imps, Tree Demons, ghommids, dewilds, genie . . .' and others). Within 'The Welcome of the Dead' there is the brittle elegance used in the Court of Mata Kharibu; the pleas, in verse, of the Dead Man and Dead Woman; the choric exchanges of the Spirits and the Half-Child; the apocalyptic threats of the Ants; the grim statements of *real politik* which come from the Triplets; and the fumblings for words and images to describe the events of the night during the 'epilogue'. Though all in English, several of these idioms, some among the most effective, draw on Yoruba modes of discourse and traditions of rhetoric.

While relying on narrative and words to a considerable extent, Soyinka also employs rites, rituals and gestures. It is clearly his intention to communicate as much through actions as through words in *A Dance of the Forests*. But, though fairly extensive, his stage-directions represent little more than jottings, and precisely what impression he wished to establish at, for instance, the conclusion of the play is not clear from the text. His production of *A Dance* at the time of Nigeria's independence did not, it seems, clarify all the obscurities, perhaps because of the problems encountered in staging this theatrical hybrid. He has indicated that he was not entirely satisfied with the work presented for independence, but he has not staged a second production.

Peter Enahoro, a distinguished journalist, was one of those who conscientiously tried to extract a meaning from the production, to penetrate the symbolism and uncover the allegory.[4] Soyinka's response to his review was revealing. In an interview, Soyinka challenged the notion that the play, any play, could or should be 'understood'. He asked that plays, his plays, should be responded to 'through the pores of the skin'; he argued that his only obligation to his audience was to provide 'exciting theatre', and asserted that he would be happy if he could 'set a riddle' which would keep audiences thinking.[5] Over the years he has argued that some people did not approach his play in the proper spirit. These were, in his terms, 'Dr PhD, or Lawyer LLB or Minister MHR' who were alienated by their European-encouraged expectations and could not submit their intellects to their senses and respond to the moods and rhythms. They were not prepared to dispense with verbal clues and trust their senses. The people who came back night after night to watch his production of *A Dance* were, Soyinka has said, the cooks and cleaners who worked on the campus at Ibadan.

Though Soyinka might like to create a theatre to which the audience responds as to, say, a festival, I don't think he succeeded in *A Dance*. There is a considerable amount of dialogue drama in *A Dance* and careful attention to the verbal clues, the revelations and the cross-questioning, is rewarding. The play's style raises expectations that attention to language will be rewarded.

The meaning of the play must be worked for and is partly conveyed through Demoke, who can be described as the protagonist. He is a complex man, creative and violent, an artist and a murderer; he is protected by Ogun, which is understandable since he combines contrasting qualities of the same order as the God of Iron. He begins to achieve tragic stature when he confesses that he killed Oremole; he confirms his status when he enters the dance and rescues the Half-Child from the hands of the malicious Eshuoro.

When Eshuoro's jester clamps the sacrificial basket onto his head, Demoke has to perform *The Dance of the Unwilling Sacrifice*, to assert himself in an ordeal on behalf of the community. He deliberately climbs the totem, although he has said he is 'a slave to heights'; he extends himself, wills himself to climb. When he falls his words from earlier in the play provide an assessment of the meaning of his descent. He had said of Oremole's death: 'There is nothing ignoble in a fall from that height. The wind cleaned him as he fell'. Despite Soyinka's talk of 'the press of the skin', these lines help the thinking, remembering, intellectualising member of the audience to understand the meaning of Demoke's achievement in climbing the totem, the effect of his fall and his purified state at the end of the ordeal. In the exchanges which conclude the play (in the 1973 text) the word 'expiation' is given particular prominence, indeed it is repeated. Some of the living, it seems, have proved and purified themselves in 'the dance'. Demoke has, it seems, 'done enough . . . felt enough for the memory of (his) remaining (life)', and Rola, when she enters, is significantly described as *chastened*. Reaching for a suitable image to describe their ordeal Demoke affirms that 'It was the same lightning that seared us through the head'. There has been 'chastening' and 'searing', ordeal and purification; there has been a working out of guilt, there has been, in short, expiation. Deeds, such as Demoke has performed, do not alter history, but they strengthen the protagonist and can purify the community; they provide an example and go some way to creating the conditions in which a new start can be made.

It is unlikely that critics will ever agree about the meaning of this play, about whether it has a meaning, or about whether the meaning should be sought through the dialogue or the dance. But a consensus may emerge over the promise and ambition which is revealed. In *A Dance*, Soyinka took up the challenge to write a full-length African tragedy for the stage and to address his countrymen at a time of 'new beginnings'. The result was an ambitious combination of elements from classical, Elizabethan, symbolist and expressionist dramas with African rites and rituals, all within a framework of festival theatre. It is the kind of unsuccessful early work out of which several successes can be carved. *A Dance* proclaimed the approach of a major dramatist.

At the very end of the play Agboreko reflects a preoccupation with divination and prophecy when he asks Demoke 'Of the future, did you learn anything?' Demoke does not reply, but the Old Man says 'When the crops have been gathered . . .' and Agboreko earns an uneasy laugh with his tag 'Proverbs to bones and silence'. Though Demoke made no prophesies, Soyinka did: he embodied them in the grim warnings of the Triplets and the Ants, and they were noticeably bleaker than those of the classical European playwrights. Soyinka gave notice that African tragic vision might on occasions be unrelieved and the prospects for Nigeria in the year of independence were grim.

5
Plays from the Sixties

Soyinka was only twenty-five when Nigeria became independent. He had been writing 'seriously' for three years and had five major plays to his credit; he was his country's leading playwright and a major figure in its literary and cultural circles. But from the nine years between the beginning of 1961 to the end of 1969 only three plays and some revue sketches have been published. The latter draw attention to an important, often neglected, body of work and one sketch, *Childe Internationale*, will be considered with the major 'plays from the sixties', *The Strong Breed, The Road* and *Kongi's Harvest*. These plays grew out of a deepening awareness of the idioms of Yoruba festivals and an intense political commitment; they exhibit a considerably more disciplined approach to playwriting than had been evidenced in *A Dance*.

The first version of *The Strong Breed* was written in the early sixties and was lost – blown off the top of a car. A year or so later, Soyinka, fortunately, found himself able to sit down and re-write the play. The seeds of *The Strong Breed*

71

were apparent, in a jumble, in 'The Dance of the Unwilling Sacrifice' at the end of *A Dance*. The play, in fact, represents an obvious strategy: return to the earlier work, extract a manageable theme and embody it in a tightly structured drama. In this case the structure is an effective combination of contrasting Nigerian rituals, *The Emperor Jones* and a passion play.

Once again the narrative is of limited interest. In *The Strong Breed*, Soyinka went to considerable lengths to scramble the chronology, so that he could control the audience's awareness of his protagonist's life and set episodes in dynamic relationships. The protagonist is Eman, a member of 'the strong breed', born in the delta region into a family charged with carrying the evil from the community to the sea in the course of a highly symbolic, annual ritual.[1] As an adolescent, he objected so strongly to the behaviour of the tutor at his initiation camp that he absconded and remained away from home for many years. He eventually returned and married, but his wife died in bearing him a son, thus experiencing the destiny of all those who give birth to sons in Eman's family, for members of 'the strong breed' 'kill' their mothers. After his young wife's funeral, Eman left home once more; he found employment in Jaguna's village, where he started to teach and established a close relationship with Sunma, Jaguna's daughter.

The play opens on the evening before the celebration of the village's annual purification ritual. For this rite, in Jaguna's village, a stranger or 'an idiot' is pressed into service, 'prepared' and driven through the streets, receiving curses and blows from the inhabitants, before being chased into the bush. In the early stages of the ceremony, Ifada, an idiot boy who has come to regard Eman as a friend, is dragged off to become the 'carrier'. Eman challenges this action and substitutes himself for the unwilling boy; during his 'preparation' for the role of 'carrier', he runs away; he is pursued through the village and Jaguna, with his henchman Oroge, decides that 'the year' will 'require' Eman's life. The 'hunters' prepare a trap for the fugitive on the path to the stream and there Eman is killed. The play closes with the villagers remorseful, Jaguna and Oroge isolated, and Sunma and Ifada united in mourning the loss of the stranger who had become their friend.

The play is based on two purification rituals – that observed in Jaguna's village and that observed in Eman's home-town – which Soyinka interlocks skilfully. There is tension in the village as the play opens, strangers are making hasty departures, Ifada has already been marked down as a possible carrier, and a child drags an effigy through the streets. The one person apparently unaffected by the deepening sense of evil is Eman, and he is the one who eventually confronts it. Once he has offered himself as a sacrifice, he is surprised: he finds the conduct of the villagers quite unlike that in his home-town. He escapes from those who are preparing him and, as he runs, hides and searches for water, episodes from his past flow into his mind and are acted out on the stage. The episodes, which provide the 'biography' of the protagonist above, fill in the background, comment on the scenes in Jaguna's village and provide a context for Eman's actions in the play. They establish particularly clearly the tension between Eman's inherited sense of responsibility to the community and his tendency to flee when confronted with testing situations.

While the rituals contribute to the dramatic tension, Soyinka has deliberately not shown us the apparently central sequence in which Eman is 'prepared' by Jaguna and Oroge. This process, presumably, involves the dulling of the senses so that the pain and humiliation of being the carrier is reduced. The playwright concentrates instead on the chase, and, even in a confined acting area, a chase, with shouts and hurtling bodies, can make exciting theatre. By contrast, the scene in which the Old Man, Eman's father, prepares for and performs his role as the carrier introduces a very different kind of tension, one which emerges from the restraint, intensity and significance of symbolic actions. The melodrama of the chase is effectively set against the spiritual ordeal of the Old Man, almost literally, shouldering responsibility.

The Strong Breed is a serious play of considerable substance, it shows a moment of spiritual growth in a community and provides excellent theatre. Eman brings the growth, for when faced by moral choices he rises to the occasion and sacrifices himself for his convictions. He insults the men of the village and ridicules the practice of using a vulnerable and unwilling carrier. He argues that 'the spirit of a new year (will not be) fooled' by an unwilling carrier. Challenged to be 'a man' himself and discovering that Jaguna has captured Ifada, he offers himself: he becomes a willing sacrifice. In this there are deliberate parallels to the self-sacrifice of Christ and of the Yoruba deity Obatala, and the drama takes on the qualities of a passion play. From the reaction of the villagers it is clear that Eman's sacrificial death has an impact on the community. The final mood indicates that a climax has been reached and passed, those who have been part of it will never be the same again. This new year provides opportunities for a new beginning in Jaguna's village.

The Strong Breed stands at the centre of Soyinka's concept of drama. In its concern with ritual and the movement through time there is a continuation of his search for African forms to combine with the traditions of dialogue drama. In the protagonist there is the embodiment of an idiosyncratic tragic hero, a man who enters the dance, 'the chthonic realm', asserts himself – in this case he rescues a 'half-child' – and, to some extent, purifies the community. The play carries on the debate with the Euro-American tradition (through inviting contrasts and comparisons with *The Emperor Jones*) and demonstrates how drama can be used to provide positive roles for emulation. It broadens the consciousness and stimulates the consciences of those who read or watch it.

During the early sixties, Soyinka made a film of part of *The Strong Breed*. He cut out the scenes relating to Eman's past and the final encounter with the Old Man, and included shots of the preparation of Eman as carrier. These alterations were, almost certainly, because of the limited film-time available, rather than for aesthetic considerations. In the conventions of the cinema, particularly in the flash-back, cross-cut, dissolve and close-up, Soyinka saw a means of transferring the idioms of Yoruba theatre and the recurrent concerns of his artistic sensibility into a permanent and widely accessible form.

During the sixties the film industry in Nigeria was, however, in its infancy, and Soyinka did not often have access to the means for producing films. He did, however, have the resources to put on plays, and, as political tension increased and censorship became more widespread, he used the stage to make pungent and relevant comments. The revue sketch, that most flexible and immediate of dramatic forms, was the means he chose for his most direct observations. Most of his sketches were so topical and so precisely aimed that they are largely of historical interest today. One, however, more of a one-act play than a sketch, contained a general truth while making a specific statement and it has been widely produced over the years in African schools and colleges. Reputedly written in forty minutes in response to a request for a short piece, it draws attention to the amusing and accessible – and barbed – work which Soyinka wrote during a time of political crises.

Childe Internationale was 'triggered' by the behaviour, real, rumoured or imagined, of the pupils at an international secondary school which had just been opened on the campus at Ibadan, and where Soyinka's wife, Laide, taught.[2] It catches and effectively conveys concern about attitudes and conduct which was current at the time.

Kotun, a self-made businessman with political aspirations and conservative tendencies, is married to a 'Been-to', a woman, that is to say, who has spent some time in London and has picked up some English habits. These include an affected accent which causes her to pronounce Yoruba words in an English manner. Their daughter, Titi, is due home on holiday from an international school and this prompts the 'Been-to' to make a special effort to introduce English ways into the domestic arrangements: she serves her husband a mixed grill, requests that he eats it with a knife and fork and asks him to summon Godwin, the house-boy, with a bell – not a yell.

Provoked by the behaviour of his daughter, Kotun eventually decides that firm action has to be taken when, after he has refused to give permission for her to have a birthday party, she says: 'Oh don't be so silly daddy'. The enraged father abandons his plans to go to a meeting and sets about putting his house in order. He makes his wife beat Titi and he commands Godwin, at the top of his voice, to 'Bring second course' – a proper Nigerian meal will, no doubt, be served.

The strength of the playlet lies in the accuracy and detail of the observation, the exposure of the affected English ways of the 'Been-to' and of the disrespectful, 'American-international' style of Titi. Kotun's rage is occasionally expressed in exhausted puns: (Titi: 'Oh isn't he such a square? . . .' Kotun: 'Well I don't care whether I am a square or a circle . . .'). But he is capable of ferocious and attractive sarcasm: 'I tell you what we ought to do. I will bring (your grandfather) down – in an iron cage – and bring him to your school. Then your friends can pay a penny a time to see him.' This sarcasm is hugely enjoyed by African audiences and the vigour of the political ensures that even an actor of moderate ability can make a decisive mark in the role.

Childe Internationale grew out of a specific situation, but it has a general significance in contemporary Africa. The text, with its references to the Beatles and to a production of *Ubu Roi*, is firmly located in the Ibadan of the early sixties, but the forces it is concerned with are at work all over Africa. Indeed they are somewhat similar to those Soyinka had already embodied in *The Lion and the Jewel*. In this case, as is appropriate in a revue sketch or one-act play, the issues are simplified and the author's sympathies crystal clear. Kotun, with his firm sense of the behaviour appropriate in a young girl and his determination to have the upper hand in his own house, is a conservative and, some would argue, a domineering Yoruba 'of the old school'. Perhaps surprisingly, he undoubtedly has Soyinka's support and, with his scorn and invective, the 'angry old man' has won the sympathy of audiences throughout Anglophone Africa.

The play was received with delight at its first performances and it has gone on giving pleasure. Although there are few international schools, almost all secondary schools in Africa expose pupils to the 'international' youth culture, and, although the Yoruba tend to place particular emphasis on the modes of address appropriate for the young to adopt to their seniors, all African communities are concerned about these issues. When I produced this play in Malawi, I found it sprang quickly to life on the stage and kept its audiences delighted from start to finish.

By contrast with *Childe Internationale, The Road* has rarely been performed, is regarded as obscure and had a long gestation. Soyinka described it as 'based on . . . a personal intimacy with a certain aspect of the road . . .'. It concerns, he said, 'a search into the essence of death.'[3]

This statement, like others which the playwright has made about the meaning of this and other of his plays, should be read with respect, but should not be regarded as the final word. In a programme note to the 1984 Chicago production, he emphasied the centrality and inevitable frustration of Professor's search in rather different terms. He described Professor as wishing 'to penetrate the very heart of phenomena'. The old man is, he wrote, seeking a categorical certainty which is alien to a Yoruba world view, a world view rooted in 'the very indeterminacy of Truth.' Professor, he continued, regards Murano, 'the human vessel which was trapped "in transition", . . . (as) a critical medium of understanding . . . the final door to the heart of phenomenon.' Professor discovers, and it is a discovery which costs him his life, that, in the words of Soyinka's rather convoluted prose, 'the community which he, in effect, appropriates and opposes to the one which casts him out proves, in the end, just as controlled and restricted by orthodox acceptances as the former.' That is to say, perhaps, that his quest leads him to alienate first the church and then the devotees of Ogun, Say Tokyo Kid amongst them.

The narrative interest of *The Road* is provided by two converging lives, those of Professor and Kotonu, which are finally brought together by a being, who seems to be only half alive, another 'half-child', Murano. In the course of the play, and by diverse techniques, we learn that Professor was, in his youth, a crusader who waged a holy war against palm-wine bars. Later he became a prominent lay-reader with a penchant for controversy and a tendency to self-advertising behaviour. Then, having stolen some of the church's money, he left the fold. At the time the play is set, he earns his living by forging licences and by selling the pickings from motor accidents, some of which he causes by uprooting road-signs. Professor is a scavenger and a wrecker; he is corrupt and wicked, confused and bewildered, part wise man and part fool.

Kotonu, the son of a truck-pusher, is a driver by profession. He used to be an excellent driver according to his effervescent 'tout' or conductor, Samson, but he was always slightly unusual. He would not, for example, deliberately run over dogs, as other drivers did in the belief that Ogun would accept the dogs as sacrifices and 'protect his own'. Kotonu's experiences shortly before the play opens include his *Narrow Escape at the Rotten Bridge*, which is presented as a flash-back, and his *Accident at the Drivers' Festival*, also presented on stage. It seems that, having been saved from death at the rotten bridge by 'a miracle', he had knocked down an *egungun* figure, Murano, who was taking part in a drivers' festival. Kotonu had managed to hide the injured dancer in his truck and had put on Murano's masquerade costume to mislead the celebrants. Blinded and 'maddened' by the blood which covered the inside of the mask, he had danced wildly to the delight of the drivers. When the festival was over, he made his escape, tossed the costume into his truck, and drove to Professor's Aksident Store. There he withdrew into himself, bewildered, unable to make any sense of the extraordinary series of events that had happened to him. The injured Murano was nursed back to health by Professor,

79

and returned to a previous occupation as a palm-wine tapper. He has not, however, regained his power of speech, perhaps because, having been knocked down while impersonating an ancestor or god, he knows secrets he must not reveal. This, at least, is what Professor thinks and he uses Murano in his search into the meaning of death in the hope of cheating fear by foreknowledge.

The dramatic convention employed in *The Road* is extremely flexible and original. From the previous paragraphs it is clear that Soyinka communicates a great deal about the events which lie behind the play. Once again the 'new' action represents only the 'tip of the iceberg' and once again we are not *told* about the past, we are *shown* it. The style is one which combines Naturalism with Symbolism, popular comedy with ritual, political satire with choral interludes, and Shakespearean echoes with absurdist mannerisms. As is inevitable with such a mixture, there is no consensus as to what the play means, indeed, as with *A Dance*, it is not a play to be understood but to be experienced. It does not reach any conclusions, it is content to take us through an ordeal, to take us a little bit further along 'the road of life' – the original title of the play – and to leave us at the end emotionally exhausted.

The setting locates the play very precisely. In the shadow of a church, beside the remains of a mammy truck which serves as the 'Aksident Store', lies Professor's 'office' and the 'home' of the lorry-park layabouts, thugs, touts and drivers. Murano is the first to wake at the beginning of the play and, taking his climbing-rope and gourd, he sets off, his purpose clearly being to tap palm-wine. Samson is the next to stir and, as the clock strikes five, he stretches. He quickly establishes himself as a comic character by his cautious approach to the church-yard, his terror at the striking of the half–hour – only moments after the hour has struck – and his ineffectual, defiant fist-shaking at the tower. Samson then fails in his attempts to wake some of the denizens of the lorry-park; he pokes at a spider's web and throws himself on his mat – only to leap up as the clock strikes yet again. The setting appears naturalistic enough, yet there are strange and symbolic dimensions to it, particularly to the church, clock and spider's web, which are made clear in the course of the play. The social significance of the church is revealed, 'na high society, . . . Politics no get dramatic passam'. So too is its importance for an earlier phase of Professor's quest: he recalls that 'on the broad span of the eagle's outstretched wings rested the Word.' The services, organ music and lights of the church add a religious dimension to the play and provide emotional colouring at various points in the drama.

While the church stands symbolically and actually in the background to the religious concerns of the play, the mammy truck is a shrine for a different religion: it is a store-house of relics from the road. These include not only the 'Spare plugs, fuses, petrol cover,/Windscreen wiper, twin carburettor./Tyre chassis hub or tie rod . . .' and the other items which customers come looking for, but also an Ogun mask and a complete masquerade figure. The truck is the tiring-house for the dancer who performs at the drivers' festival; a performer who, in a sense, *becomes* Ogun, lord of the road, and who dances to the rhythm of another deity of the way, Agemo.

The spider's web comes to represent the roads, the horrifyingly dangerous roads of Nigeria, which are traps to ensnare unwary travellers. In the course of the play, Samson draws attention to the kinship between the spider and Kotonu, both survive on the misfortune of those who have 'crashed'.

The area occupied by the stage is a place of refuge,

business and celebration. It is a 'home' without women, a shelter for the victims of nation building, for those who have drifted to the city, for those whom the city has 'kicked in the small of the back'. Nigeria is notorious for its slums and filth, and by setting his play where he does Soyinka constantly reminds audiences of these realities. He emphasises, however, that the men who gather outside the 'Aksident Store' are not without feelings or means of self-expression: they mark the events of the day by singing dirges and war-songs which add particular experiences and emotional dimensions to the play in production.

The layabouts, under their 'cap'n', Say Tokyo Kid, 'earn' money and marijuana by 'thugging' for politicians, and so the arrival at the 'Aksident Store' of Chief-in-Town on a recruiting drive is perfectly natural. Once he has got Chief-in-Town on stage, Soyinka is able to use him to comment on the depravity of politicians and the violence of politics in Nigeria. The cut and bleeding who stagger 'home' from the thugging expedition provide a comment on Nigerian politics during the mid-sixties which needs no verbal underlining. The 'Aksident Store' is an obvious place for a policeman, Particulars Joe, who includes it in his rounds. He is also drawn there by the prospect of smoking marijuana and of making enquiries into the whereabouts of an *egungun* masquerader missing after a Drivers' Festival. It is also Professor's place of business, the office in which he consults, carries out his research and forges the licences which confuse the police.

From this it is clear that Soyinka has found a quintessentially Nigerian setting, a meeting point for different groups and for the mingling of experiences. It is furthermore, a place for ritual celebrations. Each evening, Professor serves palm-wine in a version of the communion rite which complements the service held in the church. In the closing moments of *The Road*, he stages an unusual experiment as Murano puts on his *egungun* costume and dances to the music, supplied by the 'layabouts', of *Agemo emerging from the bowels of earth*.

Yet Soyinka was still dissatisfied, he wanted to bring an even greater variety of levels of meaning into his play. To do this he gave two of his characters particular qualities and, when it suited him, used flashbacks. From Professor's background it is clear that he is a man who has moved between 'worlds', between social environments and cosmological systems. When he enters, dressed in *Victorian outfit – tails, top-hat, etc*, it is clear that he belongs to a separate 'world' from the 'habitués' who surround him. As an emblem of his religion he carries a road-sign with the word 'Bend' on it. Professor, the adopted title indicates that he is an expert, lives in a world in which the mundane and the metaphysical are inextricably entwined. He moves between these two levels of reality without effort, unaware that for most people the planes are separated. For instance, Professor can ask, without any sense that it is an extraordinary question: 'Do (the dead) give overdrafts . . .?' His elision of the two planes is apparent in almost all of his speeches: its particular quality of transforming the ordinary into the transcendental is presented with the utmost clarity in his preparation of Kotonu's account of how the mammy truck overtook his vehicle just before the Accident at the Rotten Bridge. Kotonu says: 'It was a full load and it took some moments overtaking us, heavy it was.' Professor, *writing furiously*, imparts a metaphysical dimension to his account. He writes: 'It dragged alongside and after an eternity it pulled to the front swaying from side to side, pregnant with stillborns.'

The other character who moves easily from one plane to another is Samson. He has an histrionic talent and takes a delight in dressing-up, giving impersonations, telling stories with sound effects or, in the idiom of the play, 'making cinema-show'. Occasionally Samson gets 'carried away', trapped by his impersonation or even, perhaps, possessed, but most of the time he is fully aware of what he is doing and just enjoys performing. Soon after the play opens he pretends to be an African millionaire in a charade which contains social comment, a cynical assessment of the situation ('. . . man wey get money get power'), and hyperbolic statements which fuse the sacred and mundane. ('I go chop the life so tey God go jealous me. And if he take jealousy kill me I will go start bus service between heaven and hell.') Through Samson the audience also sees *The Day Professor Fought with the Bishop, How I Failed to Learn to Drive, Sergeant Burma at the Remembrance Day Service* and *How I Earned the Title "King of Touts"*. In the case of the Serjeant Burma charade there is a feeling that he may have been sucked further into the imitation than he intended. As he tears off Serjeant Burma's uniform, he prays to God to forgive him for 'fooling around pretending to be a dead man.'

Soyinka had not hesitated in earlier plays to bring the past onto the stage, so it is not surprising to find that in *The Road* there are sequences when actors present episodes which happened before the play began. The two sequences which can be described as flash-backs are 'The Narrow Escape at the Wooden Bridge' and 'The Drivers' Festival'. Kotonu and Samson are drawn into the first while Professor is writing out the report of the accident. With a shout from Samson and *a violent screech of brakes*, the two men are suddenly back at the broken bridge, with great intensity *they skirt an area carefully and peer down a hole in the ground*. Professor's occasional comments do not impinge upon them as they re-live the past. The second sequence from the past begins with the *explosive fall of the tailboard* and a lighting change. It brings before the audience the full crisis of the Drivers' Festival, and shows us how, to save himself from being attacked for knocking down 'a god', Kotonu put on the Ogun mask and, blinded by the wet blood, danced until he collapsed.

When *The Road* was first produced it bewildered many of the critics. Some recognised its vitality, some even appreciated the way in which it worked through atmosphere, and how, as a 'mystical-satirical' drama, it had 'one foot in the limbo of dissolving flesh that is called *agemo* and the other firmly up the rump of modern Nigeria.'[4] Since then critics have tended to concentrate on the socio-economic analysis in the play, what Biodun Jeyifo calls 'The Hidden Class-Struggle', or the metaphysical element, the meaning of 'The Word'.[5] Commentaries have tended to be made on the basis of literary analyses rather than theatrical experience, and this has led to confusion and distortion.

In 1978 Derek Bullock directed the play with boys from Government College, Kano, and it was performed at the University of Ibadan. The production was not perfect: the set did not fit the Arts Theatre Stage, the music and dance elements had not been adequately worked out and the cast was uneven. However, Funso Alabi as Samson and Bullock as Professor were outstandingly good and the play made a tremendous impact. The audience was held throughout; responsive laughter greeted humour which, in reading the text, I thought was rather laboured. The details of the society which the playwright submitted for the attention of the audience, the confusions and contradictions, the extravagances of style, were greeted with delighted recognition. The conflict between Say Tokyo Kid and Professor was clearly established, for the captain of the thugs, despite his American gangster accent, was obviously deeply conservative and intensely religious. His conviction that 'there is a hundred spirits in every guy of timber trying to do you down cause you've trapped them in' was indicated by the reassurance he derived from his talisman. He was clearly suspicious of Professor's manipulation of Murano in his quest to find out about death.

The rhythm of the production built up firmly. The violent confrontation at the end of Part One, in which Murano twisted his climbing-rope around Salubi's neck, effectively prepared for the violence at the end of the play. The Drivers' Festival, in which there was both violence and a dance in which the dancer collapsed exhausted, also established a sequence which it was satisfying to see repeated. When the drama drew to a close, Professor's last speech, 'Be even like the road itself,' passed for almost nothing, it was the music and, particularly, the spinning masquerade which held attention and established the mood in which the audience, deeply satisfied, left the auditorium. The following morning it was possible to perceive weaknesses in the production, but it was not possible to forget the power of the experience which Bullock and his cast had unleashed from Soyinka's text.

The lesson to draw from this is that it is necessary to stand back from Soyinka's words in order to appreciate the stage images he creates and the patterns into which his plays fall. In this case it is important to see Professor's death in the context provided by a series of scenes about his past and by the gathering strength of ritual forces. Sensitivity to these qualities means that preoccupations with narrative, class analysis and the meaning of 'the Word' are replaced by an experience of Soyinka's play in performance. Despite similarities with that of others, his theatre is distinctive both in its conventions and its intentions. Its distinctiveness is

1. *The Lion and the Jewel,* Royal Court Theatre, 1966. Femi Euba as Lakunle and Hannah Bright Taylor as Sidi.

2. *The Lion and the Jewel,* Royal Court Theatre, 1966.

3. *The Trials of Brother Jero*, Bristol University Drama Dept, 1974.

4. *The Trials
of Brother Jero*,
Bristol University
Drama Dept,
1974.

5. *The Strong Breed*, Chancellor College, Malawi, 1976. Anthony Nazombe as Eman.

6. The University of Malawi's Travelling Theatre production of *Childe Internationale, 1979*, Villah Ngwira as Titi, Evelyn Kanwijolo as her mother.

7. *Kongi's Harvest* Wole Soyinka as Kongi. Directed by Ossie Davis for Omega / Calpenny Films 1970.

8. Wole Soyinka with actors from *The Road*, 1972.

9. *The Road*, Theatre Royal, Stratford East, London, 1965. Horace James (Professor) Dapo Adelugba (Murano) and Alton Kamala (Say Tokyo Kid).

10. *The Road* Goodman Theatre, Chicago 1984.

11. *The Bacchae of Euripides.* National Theatre, 1973.
Martin Shaw as Dionysus and John Shrapnel as Pentheus.

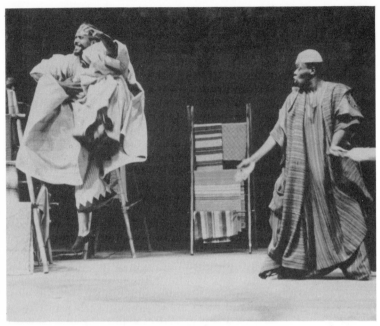

12. Norman Matlock and Ben Halley in *Death and the King's Horsemen*, The Goodman Theatre, Chicago 1984.

13. *Opera Wonyosi* The University of Ife Theatre and Students 1977.

partly to be found in the specifically Yoruba attitudes and conventions which it employs and for this reason it may be described as 'African'.

Soyinka said that his next play, *Kongi's Harvest*, was 'inspired entirely by a sentence which (he) once heard an African leader pronounce "I want him back alive, if possible"'.[6] *Kongi's Harvest* also grew out of Soyinka's concern with human rights and political liberties, out of his conviction that the role of political activist was an important and honourable one, out of his perception of political developments on the continent of Africa and out of his anxiety to root his theatre in the idioms of African festival performances.

In African festival theatre the narrative element is often buried and digging it up does not necessarily enrich the experience of participants. A preoccupation with plot can obscure the larger issues raised by a play based on a festival, but it is still useful to establish what, in a narrative sense, happens in *Kongi's Harvest*. The play is set in the imaginary African state of Isma during the preparations for, celebration and aftermath of a New Yam Festival. The ruler of Isma, Kongi, is a repressive, ambitious autocrat, who is assisted by a ubiquitous Organizing Secretary, advised by a fraternity of largely sycophantic Aweris and enthusiastically supported by a brutal Carpenters' Brigade. He has put some of his most powerful opponents, including Oba Danlola, into detention, but he has not, as the opening sequence, 'Hemlock', makes clear, quelled the Oba's ebullient and independent opposition. Kongi's rule is also challenged by his ex-mistress, the mysterious and beautiful Segi, by her female supporters and by Daodu, Danlola's much-travelled nephew and heir who is the leader of a successful farming co-operative. The dictator wants to usurp Danlola's position; specifically he wants to receive the new yam from the Oba's hands at the New Yam Festival and, by eating part of it, to present himself to the people as their protector and spiritual leader. Danlola is understandably unwilling to abdicate his religious functions by co-operating in this image-making exercise, but Segi and Daodu are anxious that he should at least pretend to co-operate in order to draw Kongi to the public celebration of the New Yam Festival. There they plan to have him assassinated just as the New Yam is presented to him, just when he is about to commit an outrageous blasphemy.

In the course of the play, plans are discussed and move forward: Danlola is persuaded to acceed to Kongi's request and Kongi agrees to release some political prisoners. A detail of the assassination plot is changed slightly when Segi's father escapes from detention and takes on the role of marksman. But, before he can kill Kongi, he is himself shot. In an 'improvised' denouement to Part Two, Segi dances in accompanied by her women supporters, and presents Kongi with her father's severed head. As Kongi stares at it aghast, the lights go out. This is followed by 'Hangover' from which it seems that, despite the shock which the system has received, Kongi remains in control.

Some of this story, and some of the most exciting elements such as the plan to shoot Kongi, can be easily missed at a first reading of the play and many have come out of performances thoroughly confused about what was going on in terms of 'the plot'. What makes an impact on all is the Yam Festival. The play builds up to that celebration; much of the dialogue is about preparation for it and the most spectacular scene is the festival itself – or an improvisation based on it. Soyinka has found an idiom for this piece in the celebration of the New Yam Festival; the image of the New Yam and the songs which celebrate it provide a cultural and dramatic context for the working out of his ideas.

Yet, though it looms large, Kongi's planned violation of the New Yam Festival is not unique. It is merely one of several occasions on which he has challenged the authority of Danlola and abrogated to himself the spiritual rights of the Oba. For the opposition, the Festival provides an occasion when the paranoid Kongi is out in the open and can be hit by an assassin's bullet. To strike him down at a moment when he is violating a taboo is a refinement which will win friends for the plotters. The play, inevitably, contains a great deal more than the Festival, and when this extra material is studied it reveals that Soyinka has employed techniques which have become familiar from the examination of previous plays: these include careful attention to comparison and contrast, but not, in this instance, shifts into the past.

The opening scene, 'Hemlock', shows Danlola in detention: the leader under the old dispensation has been placed behind barbed wire by the new. The khaki uniforms and detention camp regulations speak volumes about Kongi's regime and by showing us these things Soyinka saves hundreds of words. The Oba's poetic, musical, richly dressed retinue, vivacious despite Danlola's captivity, places before the audience an image of the old order 'in durance vile'. Danlola himself is warm, witty, mischievous, dignified: Soyinka has made him sympathetic, while refusing to sentimentalise him.

In the course of 'Hemlock', there is a moment of particular tension when, in the middle of a praise song for Danlola, the Superintendent *seizes the lead drummer by the wrist* and *everything stops*. After a pause, and in the *complete silence* which follows, Danlola asks with great deliberation: 'You stopped the royal drums?' The interruption of the ceremonies of the Oba is not, Danlola makes clear, the first, nor will it be the last. Indeed, it looks back to the imprisoning of Danlola and anticipates both the bursting of Danlola's drum by Daodu and the interruption of the New Yam Festival.

Danlola is, it is apparent, not completely at the Superintendent's mercy, and in order to show this he *makes a motion as if he means to prostrate himself* before the 'slave in khaki'. The Superintendent is sufficiently affected by the attitudes of the community in which he was reared to beg the Oba not to reverse the appointed order by prostrating before him. The recognition of the honour due to Danlola by the Superintendent is contrasted in the scenes which follow with the over-weaning ambition of Kongi, who thinks it right and proper that the Oba should hand the New Yam to him. The enormity of this demand is made clear by the exchanges and gestures in 'Hemlock' between Danlola and the Superintendent. Even if we come to the play ignorant of the respect due to Yoruba Obas this scene provides information about expected attitudes and behaviour.

In Part One of the play the little action that there is moves forward slowly as the audience's attention is switched back and forth between Kongi's Mountain Retreat and Segi's Night Club. The stage direction indicates that both sets *are present on different parts of the stage and are brought into play in turn, by lights*, an arrangement which is ideal for making contrasts. In the mountain retreat, against the background of a chant in honour of Kongi, the Aweris bicker and squabble as they endeavour to manufacture an image for the dictator. There are topical allusions, and, through the Fifth Aweri whose independence and spirit separate him from the others, Soyinka makes fun of the 'algebraic quantums' in Nkrumah's *Consciencism*. In the Retreat, the atmosphere is sterile, the jargon barren, the image-making synthetic; it is perfectly appropriate that the Aweris should be starved for it is clear they are working for a negative, life-denying force.

When Kongi appears he is fearful, power-crazed and forgetful. 'How dead?' he says at one point, 'I don't remember condemning any of them to death.' He is also, and in this he is to be compared and contrasted with Danlola, a performer, one who seeks to achieve particular effects. But whereas Danlola plays his role magnificently, Kongi is seen struggling to get the emphases right, for instance he labours over the placing of the stress on the line 'I am the spirit of harvest'. He never succeeds because he is not that Spirit. He aspires to roles for which he is unsuited, dresses himself in 'borrowed robes', tries to invoke a spirit which rightly belongs to someone else. In one sequence, the Organizing Secretary confides that he has 'reason to believe' that a press photographer might find his way into Kongi's retreat. Kongi protests, and, in a manner which exposes him as a fraud and hypocrite, strikes poses in which, shades of Nkrumah once more, he presents himself as a second Christ. During the brief scene in the retreat which closes the First Part, Kongi, frantic at the news that some detainees have escaped, uses almost the very words which 'triggered' the play: 'I want him back – alive if possible . . .'. And then, as a comment on his condition, he falls into an epileptic fit. In this instance, as in many others, Soyinka uses action to speak louder – and more clearly – than words.

Kongi and his drab advisors in their austere retreat are sharply contrasted with Danlola and the vivacity with which Danlola's supporters enliven the detention camp. In Part One, Soyinka establishes Segi's Club as a third point in the political, social and emotional landscape of Ismaland. The Club has coloured lights and a *juju band guitar gone typically mad*, there is dancing and drinking, and a conspiratorial air. The Organizing Secretary, whom Kongi has made responsible for the arrangements concerning the New Yam Festival, is nervous and out of place in the Night Club. Brisk and business-like, he brings the chill of the Aweris' Retreat into the life-assertive Club, which belongs to Segi, a woman, a *femme fatale*, an inspiration and an enigma. The lyrics of a song in her honour establish the mystery of the lady: 'The being of Segi/Swirls the night/ In potions round my head'. Segi is one of a line of 'super women' in Soyinka's plays which stretches back to Rola/ Madam Tortoise and even to Sidi, all 'right cannibal(s) of the female species'. She is not a 'round' character but she fulfils an important dramatic function: she establishes that the female principle supports the opposition to dictatorship and, on occasions, leads it.

Daodu fits into an even more familiar tradition in Soyinka's drama: that of the young male protagonist. He is presented as an admirable contender for leadership: through his father, Sarumi, and through Danlola, he has a legitimate claim to leadership under the 'traditional' system, and he also has wide experience of the world, having recently 'returned from everywhere'. Daodu has demonstrated his powers of leadership and his ability to promote fecundity by his position in the farming settlement which has produced the largest new yam. He is associated with music, poetry, the creative use of words (he coins slogans with ease) and with Segi. He is the true Spirit of Harvest, and, guided by Segi, he preaches Life. Indeed he embodies the life-force, or, at least, he is intended to. Once again the dramatic function a character is required to fulfil is more impressive than the character.

The Second Part of *Kongi's Harvest* begins as the play itself had begun, with Danlola in fine form. He is finding excuses for not attending the New Yam Festival, and before he does in fact leave for the festival the tension builds up, with Daodu hinting at the plans that he and Segi have laid and which will fall through if the Festival is not held. When the scene shifts to the New Yam celebrations, the Carpenters' Brigade sing of their loyalty – and then reveal their fascist inclinations by giving Nazi salutes. Dende, a member of Danlola's household who has defected to the Brigade, provides some wit and wisdom, and the Secretary learns to his dismay that Segi has been elected leader of the Women's Corps. The excitement builds up through singing, dancing and the tension apparent in leading characters. Daodu delivers a speech in which he denounces Kongi as a 'messiah of pain' and identifies himself as a messiah of abundance, joy and life. Danlola offers the New Yam to Kongi, but as the autocrat places his hand over it in benediction (how often benedictions feature at key points in Soyinka's plays) there is a burst of gun-fire. But it is not Kongi who is hit. Out of the confusion which follows, it emerges that Segi's father, the substitute assassin, has been killed. Segi refuses to give way to grief and, saying she is 'tired of being the mouse in (Kongi's) cat-and-mouse game', sets off to improvise a fitting denouement to the festival. Kongi makes his speech; he *exhorts, declaims, reviles, cajoles, damns, curses, vilifies, excommunicates, execrates*, but the sound of the revelry rises and drowns his words. He is reduced to a gesticulating, sweating figure, foaming in the background, possessed by a Spirit of Hate. When Segi moves she manages to take Kongi by surprise and makes a muffled symbolic statement about the regime by presenting Kongi with the severed head of her father.

In the epilogue, 'Hangover', certain of the characters respond to the cataclysm of the festival and the sound effects hint at the next development. The 'hornets nest/Is truly stirred'; there are plans afoot to bundle Daodu and Segi out of the country if they are not already in Kongi's hands. The Secretary makes for the border; Dende, we are assured, will 'do much/As the wind directs', and Danlola sets off to hasten Daodu's departure. The royal anthem rises and plays for a short while, then the sound of an iron grating is heard: it *descends and hits the ground with a loud, final clang*. The implications are that Kongi's rule asserts itself more repressively than ever.

Though Daodu and Segi have failed in their plan to remove the dictator and life has been defeated by death, the final mood is not one of total despair. The plotters had known that failure was likely, almost inevitable; encouragement should be drawn from their determination to do what they believed was right despite the knowledge of almost certain failure. Their activism is contrasted with the pathetic resignation expressed by the Secretary, and, significantly, is approved by Danlola, who confesses that he 'drank from the stream of madness/For a little while'. Soyinka does not delude himself, or allow his play to delude those working for change, into thinking that it is easy to overthrow tyranny. He encourages enterprising opposition: gestures of defiance are never to him 'mere gestures' and should always be made. The man dies, Soyinka later wrote in his prison notes, in all who keep silent in the face of tyranny. The man in Daodu – and the woman in Segi – live.

These, at least, appear to be the implications of the published text. The version used for the first production was significantly different and, in Soyinka's productions, 'Hangover' has generally been cut. Indeed, Soyinka has frequently shown a willingness to cut and alter his scripts drastically in production. In the script for the first production there was no gun-fire and Danlola presented the yam to Segi, presumably to avoid giving it to Kongi and, perhaps, to acknowledge the formidable power she wields. In the anti-military Ife production (1971) the end was marked by the ascent of a flotilla of gas-filled balloons. In Soyinka's film-script, which is significantly different from the play-text at several points, the assassination is successful and the final image is of Segi's father and the leader of the Carpenters' Brigade bargaining for power.[7] These changes show Soyinka as playwright-producer revising and re-working his script aware that it is to be performed before a particular audience at a particular time and anxious to make a decisive and relevant impact.

I am not, however, convinced that *The Presentation of the Severed Head* can ever make an effective contribution to this drama. My objections to the severed head begin on the level of stage-craft: it is difficult to make a convincing property head. Even if one is manufactured, it is not certain that the audience will recognise what it is. If they recognise what it is, they will be confused as to whose it is. If they guess whose it is they may be at a loss as to what it means. Some, encouraged by the references to a new messiah in Daodu's speech (lines which were, apparently, cut for the performance in Dakar during 1966) have seen the gesture in terms of Salome's presentation of John the Baptist's head to Herod. But, the implications of this analogy are only partly helpful, and reference to James Frazer's *Golden Bough* or Soyinka's *Aké* are as good, if not better, points of departure for the analyst. In those books we read that a newly installed Alake had to consume a part of his predecessor's body in order to establish the legitimacy of his succession. Are we to suppose that Segi is inviting Kongi to establish a ritual link with her father? Or is she, and the context of the feast makes this an attractive speculation, inviting him to become a cannibal – or even demonstrating that he has already become one? While the play as a whole seems to build up to some such interpretation, for Kongi is a harvester of death, the stage action is obscure and ambiguous.

It may be that my uncertainties would have been banished if I had seen one of Soyinka's productions, or an adequate production by another director. Unfortunately I have only seen the Accra (1970) production by George Andoh-Wilson and that did not provide the sort of controlled, choreographed approach which the text requires. It was embarked upon without Soyinka's permission and disastrously overstated a minor element in the play: through costume, gesture and choice of actor, Andoh-Wilson stressed the links between Kongi and Nkrumah. The play, presented in post-Nkrumah Ghana, became a statement of a politically expedient position; it avoided comment on contemporary issues, joined in the celebrations of anti-Nkrumahism and curried favour with the group in power. Not surprisingly, Soyinka realised how the letter of his play might be turned against its spirit and declined the royalties due to him from the production.

The critical reaction to the play has revealed the difficulties involved in writing a script which draws on contemporary politics and yet tries to embody a wider vision. Immediate reactions involved spotting the originals of the characters – one of whom was Nkrumah. This was followed by an assault on the ideology of the play: Soyinka was accused of having lent his talents to forwarding the cause of the Central Intelligence Agency. More recently critics have objected to the 'elitism' revealed by the choice of Daodu as protagonist, the 'lack of historical awareness' apparent in the play's endorsement of the role of the individual in stimulating change, and the conspicuous failure to define the political affiliations of the plotters.

Soyinka, despite the very specific and political nature of some of his satire, is concerned with attitudes rather than political blue-prints, with positions not parties. Kongi is not Nkrumah or Banda or any one else, he is a combination of the repressive, anti-life propensities which Soyinka associated with certain aspects of a breed of leaders. In a programme note to his second production he emphasised this element by writing: 'The play is not about Kongi, it is about Kongism. Therefore, while it has been suggested with some justification that there are resemblances between the character of Kongi and that of ex-President Nkrumah – the play was indeed first presented in December (August, J G), 1965, while Nkrumah was still in power – it must be emphasised that Kongism has never been dethroned in Black Africa. There are a thousand and more forms of Kongism – from the crude and blasphemous to the subtle and sanctimonious . . . All roads lead in the same direction, and down this hill, striking sparks from careless skulls, Kongi rides again.' In a letter, published in a study aid to *Kongi's Harvest* which I wrote, Soyinka indicated his awareness of Nkrumah's positive contribution to Africa. The satirical attack was, he stressed, on certain aspects of Nkrumah's leadership; it was not intended to be confused with a wholesale condemnation of the man, the Pan-Africanist. Given the characterisation of Kongi in the text, it is inevitable that links between the two will be made, at least for so long as Nkrumah's 'redeemer image' and *Consciencism* remain in the public memory. Danlola, by contrast, establishes himself from the very start as a seamless combination of individuals and as an embodiment of life-asserting values. There is evidence in the characterisation of Kongi and Danlola that Soyinka found it easier to create some sorts of characters than others, and that his concern with topicality did more harm to some of his creations than others. In conclusion, it can be said that the play's attempt to make a statement that was at once topical and timeless is only sporadically successful.

During the sixties, while creating a theatre of social and political comment, Soyinka made a sustained examination of the use of ritual and of film techniques in the theatre. The combination of them with the mystical and the satirical in the three major plays considered in this chapter is unusual and may confuse. The conventions of purification rites and African festival theatre on which he drew are unfamiliar to many of his readers and audiences, even the idea of theatre as a sharing of experience may be strange. However, for the reader who has observed the ways in which Soyinka's early plays use time, present women and protagonists, absorb styles from music and dance, and conclude at the end of a cycle, these complex dramas can be seen as the evolution of a style rather than as a revolution. Though the three plays are not without enduring obscurities and distracting ambiguities, they constitute a very substantial achievement. During the sixties, Soyinka published only a few plays, but he extended and confirmed his early promise and became a major playwright.

6
The Post—War Play

Although the Civil War dominated Soyinka's writing for a
considerable period, only a small part of the work from this
time was in dramatic form. Part of the reason for this may
be provided by the extent to which one grim drama drained
him of his bitterness and by the circumstances under which
the only published play from this period was written.
Madmen and Specialists purged the rancour and despair
which had accumulated during the months in detention and
confronted the evil which Soyinka had encountered with
fierce, acerbic humour. The text was completed from
drafts, some of which may have been made in Kaduna
Prison, at the stimulating Eugene O'Neill Center, Waterford, Connecticut, while Soyinka rehearsed with the University of Ibadan Theatre Arts Company for a sponsored
production.

Madmen continues the examination of themes present in
earlier works such as *The Strong Breed* and *Kongi's
Harvest*, bringing corrupt power into collision with humane
interests. It is set *in and around the home surgery of Dr.*

99

Bero, lately returned from the wars. Four Mendicants, Cripple, Blindman, Aafaa and Goyi, have established themselves in front of the 'home' to guard, spy, beg, entertain and comment. Dr. Bero, it emerges has come back from the wars transformed: he has exchanged his practice as a medical doctor for the sinister role of intelligence officer. His surgery has been transformed too, for in it he has secretly imprisoned his father, referred to as the Old Man. The Old Man had, we learn, opposed the war: he had challenged the war-mongers, in a manner similar to that employed by Michael Flanders and Donald Swann in 'The Reluctant Cannibal', with the argument that if you can justify war you can also justify cannibalism. The Old Man had translated this argument into a ghoulish coup-de-théâtre by arranging for members of the upper echelons of the army to consume a meal of human flesh. He had anticipated that when told what they had eaten the officers would be filled with self-disgust and compelled to reconsider their attitude to war. This did not happen, indeed the plan back-fired completely: the unscrupulous and 'power-hungry' commanders, Dr. Bero among them, delighted in what they fed on and quickly developed an appetite for human flesh.

Shortly before the play begins Bero has brought his father home under a guard made up of four of the wounded and battle-scarred, the Mendicants. These men had at one stage been on a rehabilitation programme run by the Old Man, but rather than teach them the skills usually associated with schemes for the disabled, such as mat-making and basket-weaving, the 'subversive' teacher had introduced them to his 'Cult of As', and, more important, had taught them to think. Though the Mendicants' relationship with the Old Man has altered, it still includes a degree of respect; they act out the sketches he produced with them, sing the songs he taught them and view the world with the independent, cynical attitude which he encouraged – an almost nihilistic view in which humour preserves sanity and edges aside despair. The Mendicants also spy on the Earth Mothers whose store of herbs stands to one side of the stage. They seek to learn about the herbs which the old women, with help from Dr. Bero's gentle sister, Si Bero, have gathered. As the drama unfolds it becomes clear that the Earth Mothers have great knowledge and that their collection includes both curative and poisonous herbs of considerable power. The power can be used for good or evil and the women, who, represent an earthed, age-old wisdom, are anxious that it should remain in responsible and humane hands. In the closing sequence of the play, the Old Man seems to be about to operate on Cripple; Bero shoots his father; the Earth Mothers set their collection of herbs on fire, and the Mendicants break gleefully into their favourite song, 'Bi o ti wa', until the words and lights are suddenly cut off.

The set is unchanged throughout and provides a natural and public meeting-ground for the representatives of very different forces. Behind the apparent naturalism is a significant degree of symbolism, some of it reinforced by the horizontal and vertical lines of the buildings which surround the acting area: the notion of 'levels of meaning' finds expression in the levels of the set. The surgery, where some important sequences are played, is significantly *down in a cellar*; immediately in front of this, herbs and pieces of bark are laid out to dry. To one side, in *a semi-open hut* which is the *higher structure,* sit the Earth Mothers, Iya Agba and Iya Mate, one smoking while the other tends a small fire. From the beginning these two are linked with fire, with its multiple symbolic associations, its value for cooking, its ability to give warmth and comfort, its fearsome power to destroy and its benign gift of fumigating and cleansing. The appearance and the afflictions of the Mendicants who sit by the road which runs past the surgery provide an image of the sacrifice and mutilation which war demands and leaves in its wake. When the play begins the audience should be impressed by the tableau: the women face the men; those who toil collecting herbs confront those who beg in the streets; inheritors of a tradition of herbal medicine are contrasted with the devotees of the Cult of As who are the victims and celebrants of a world where lives are cheap and where limbs are 'lost' on the roll of a dice.

The Mendicants establish the opening mood of the play with a grotesque game of chance in which the stakes are parts of their bodies. As they bicker, they convey an impression of a dehumanised, brutalised commuity. When the drama gets underway, Soyinka repeatedly makes use of the four men to comment on events, draw diverse experiences into consideration, help the plot unfold and represent the legacy of war. Almost any passage of the Mendicants' chorus-like commentary reveals their skill in creating mocking, scaberous, revealing, macabre characters. At one point they take off from the word 'dutiful'. Goyi claims Dr. Bero is 'dutiful'.

> CRIPPLE: Him a dutiful son? You're crazy.
> BLINDMAN: I know what he means. (*He points an imaginary gun.*) Bang! All in the line of duty!
> (*Goyi clutches his chest, slumps over.*)
> (*CP.II* p.220)

When the legality of this execution is challenged on the grounds the Goyi has not been tried, the victim is 'resurrected'. Aafaa (*in a ringing voice*) says 'You are *accused*' and, the requirements of the law now satisfied,

Goyi is summarily despatched once more. When, from the dead, he says he has 'no complaints', they even allow him to be buried. This grizzly sequence, with its unmistakable comment on the kind of rough and rapid 'justice' meted out by military rulers, leads, through the mention of vultures, into a series of jibes at those, such as Gowon's companions in uniforms, who claimed to be 'cleaning up the mess' left by others. Addressing an imaginary audience and with his hand on an imaginary gun, Aafaa asks: 'Is there anyone here who does not approve of us, just say so and we quit.' Predictably, and as a 'model' of military rulers in Nigeria, he is able to assure his companions that 'They insist we stay'.

While the Mendicants, and the Old Man, frequently employ pantomime to communicate their view of life, language is also used extensively and effectively. In a particularly intense speech near the end of the play the Old Man's voice rises *to a frenzy* as he tears apart words in order to show his scorn for religious and organized systems of thought which challenge his notion of 'As'

. . . You cyst, you cyst, you splint in the arrow of arrogance, the dog in dogma, tick of a heretic, the tick in politics, the mock of democracy, the mar of marxism, a tic of the fanatic, the boo in buddhism, the ham in Mohammed, the dash in the criss-cross of Christ. A dot on the i of ego, an ass in the mass, the ash in ashram, a boot in kibbutz, the pee of priesthood, the peepee of perfect priesthood, oh how dare you raise your hind-quarters you dog of dogma and cast the scent of your existence on the lamp-post of Destiny You HOLE IN THE ZERO of NOTHING! (*C.P., II*, p.275.)

The Medicants have learned from the Old Man to scrutinize and analyse language; they take words and phrases to pieces, play with them and use the broken bits as windows through which they can see the corrupt, exploitative, evil forces at work in the world.

In constructing *Madmen and Specialists*, Soyinka achieved a great degree of flexibility and fluidity without recourse to flashbacks (as in *The Road*) or shifts of location (as in *Kongi's Harvest*). The various 'slabs' of experience incorporated into the play, including the ritual chants of the Earth Mothers and the long speech in which the Priest recalls his debates with the Old Man, are set off against the swaggering of Bero and the grim cabaret of the Mendicants. The Mendicants and the Old Man provide in fact, an almost non-stop revue, a satirical and often sick contribution to the unfolding drama. Their bitterness and the speed of their attack, as illustrated by the passages examined, provide a cutting edge to the play which challenges audiences and keeps them alert. They constitute a new element in Soyinka's drama and help him to achieve a high degree of intensity in this work.

I have no doubt that the play conveys a vision which Soyinka was very anxious to communicate. Part of the vision emerges through the Mendicants, the Old Man and the use of language, part from the image of corrupted power which is presented by Bero, and part from the integrity of the uncorrupted Earth Mothers. One of the central images in the play is of cannibalism, an image of man's tendency to feed off and draw power from his fellow man. It stands at the centre of Soyinka's apprehension of man's relationship with man in this play from the tense post-Civil War Period.

In reviewing the American world premiere of *Madmen*, Alan Bunce wrote that the drama was given 'real lift and impact (by) lively outbursts of tribal chanting, acidic humour, ritual form (and) forcefully worded flights of bitter speculation'.[1] Abiola Irele, commented as follows on the Nigerian production: 'The play itself is a kind of fantasy that takes off from reality and whose action seems to run parallel to it by developing the implications of real life situations to their weird, absurd and, finally, inhuman limits. The prevailing atmosphere of the play is one of acute moral and spiritual discomfort'.[2] Soyinka's reluctance to give directors permission to produce his longer plays is justified by the two pirate productions of *Madmen and Specialists* which I have seen. Neither the Holland Park Link Group production, which I saw in London, nor the Ahmadu Bello University Studio Theatre, which I saw in Ibadan, handled the language, rhythms or visual images of the play with adequate control or sensitivity.

It is essential for a production to get below the brittle surface of this play, to expose the underlying confrontation between good and evil, and to emphasise the Old Man's challenge to the sinister forces which are represented by Bero. This the Old Man does by offering himself as a victim for his maniac son to slaughter. When Bero shoots his father, he sheds the last vestiges of his humanity, he breaks the ultimate taboo, he joins Oedipus and Isola and all those who are condemned to go through life with their father's blood on their hands. The Earth Mothers seize the opportunity offered to them, and, as the parricide stands with smoking pistol over the body of his victim, they set fire to their store of herbs in an irreversible act which will prevent their power and knowledge falling into unworthy hands.

Though the play is a bitter and violent attack on a sick society, the ending is not entirely without the prospect of improvement. The Old Man is dead, but the distraction caused by his death allows the Earth Mothers to destroy the herbs which the evil Bero had sought to possess. As the smoke billows onto the stage, it is time for a new game to start: the players are different, for the Old Man has been killed by his son and Bero stands exposed as a violator of the final taboo. The Mendicants are cut off in the line 'Even as it was' which they sang early in the play, but, despite the apparent implications of the chant, there has been change. And while there is change there is, even in the nearly despairing world of this play, hope.

Although one should avoid the error of confusing the creator with his creatures, there are significant elements which Soyinka shares with the Old Man he drew in *Madmen and Specialists*. Both are activists with a perception of the failings of their societies, both use songs, sketches and their influence over performers to proclaim their vision and expose evil. The Old Man arranged a grim banquet; Soyinka a harrowing production. In the seventies and eighties, Soyinka found occasions to provide his groups of actors, his Mendicants, with material which challenged the assumptions of Nigerian audiences.

7
The Plays of Exile

From Soyinka's first extended period away from Nigeria (1954 to 1960) came the Leeds Plays and some of the drafts which were re-worked in the Independence Plays. From his second extended exile (1971 to 1975) there are three published plays: *The Metamorphosis of Brother Jero, The Bacchae of Euripides* and *Death and the King's Horseman.* These plays drew on ideas and characters from the late fifties and early sixties: they are united by a clarity of execution which comes partly from an anxiety to make a political comment and partly from an intimate re-encounter with Greek drama.

Soyinka left Nigeria disgusted at the brutalised society which he saw around him. The Civil War had been followed by a wave of armed robberies and, providing the only sort of solution it understood, Yacubu Gowon's military regime established tribunals to try anyone accused of armed robbery. These tribunals had the power to condemn those they found guilty to public execution by firing squad. Executions of hastily tried suspects were carried out in

107

various centres in the country, many on the Bar Beach near Lagos, in a carnival atmosphere, with hawkers exploiting the situation for their own profit and the media determined to draw every drop of drama from the occasion.

Towards the middle of 1972, a member of the military junta, Bolaji Johnson, was given the task of clearing the prophets, praying churches and separatist sects from the Bar Beach. Soyinka imagined that this might be a prelude to the construction of a national execution amphitheatre with all the possibilities for making money and wielding influence which such a project entailed. Using his long familiarity with the *demi-monde* of the Bar Beach, information from Nigeria, his own ideas and his best-known stage character, Soyinka focussed his distrust of Gowon and his concern about the direction in which the country was being taken in a second Jero play.

The central character of *Jero's Metamorphosis* has moved from his *rent-troubled shack* of *The Trials* into a modest, whitewashed *office*. Through a convert, Sister Rebecca, he has obtained a sensitive file which indicates to whom, and for what reason, the Tourist Board of the City Council has awarded the monopolies in relation to the National Execution Amphitheatre to be built on the Bar Beach. The file indicates that the praying churches will be removed from the Beach and that the Salvation Army will be given the licence to operate in the Amphitheatre. Jero's plan is to weld the beach prophets into a new church, the Church of the Apostolic Salvation Army (CASA for short and to remind some people of the Mafia), and to blackmail the Tourist Board into awarding the 'spritual monopoly' to it instead of the Salvation Army.

The play opens with Jero dictating invitations to his fellow prophets asking them to attend a meeting. This scene provides exposition and introduces Rebecca, previously a confidential secretary with the Tourist Board; Ananias, a wrestler turned prophet with whose criminal activities Jero is well acquainted, and a posse of Tourist Board officials in search of the missing file. The scene builds up to an action-packed climax in which violence and religious ecstasy are happily combined.

In the second scene we are re-introduced to the gullible Chief Messenger from the earlier play, Chume, and discover that during his confinement in the lunatic asylum following *The Trials* he had become a trumpeter in a Salvation Army band. On the day during which the play is set, Chume's usual trumpet teacher has been replaced by Major Silva whose approach to music is rigid, foreign and uncompromising. When Jero enters, Chume is initially hostile towards his persecutor, but the promise of a place among the 'brotherhood' of prophets has the desired effect and the trumpeter is recruited to lead the brass band which is to be a feature of CASA's organization. It is clear that Chume's musical style will blend very happily with CASA's syncretistic and Yoruba-influenced approach.

The final scene opens on the prophets who have assembled at Jero's invitation, a fascinating collection of rogues and hypocrites. Ananaias is there; so is Caleb, an intellectual drunkard; Isaac, quick-witted and acerbic; Matthew, lecherous and probably a rapist, and Shadrach, the stiff-necked leader of the twenty-thousand strong Shadrach-Medrach-Abednego Apostolic Trinity. When Jero eventually arrives, he manages to enlist all except Shadrach in his spiritual army and to blackmail the Tourist Office, in the person of the Chief Executive Officer, to grant CASA the spiritual monopoly at the Execution Amphitheatre. After the new army has marched off 'to fight the good fight' and remove the shacks of the prophets, 'General' Jeroboam, in full uniform, sits at the desk beneath a photograph of himself and declares: 'After all, it is the fashion to be a desk General.'

Jero's Metamorphosis looks back not only to *The Trials* but also to the revue sketches of the mid-sixties in that it is directed at a specific social issue; it is another of what Soyinka calls his 'shot-gun pieces'. But it is more substantial than many of his directly political writings and more subtle; it embodies the 'iron fist in the velvet glove' approach. On the surface there is much to divert and entertain, an abundance of verbal wit, a gallery of vivid characters who tumble over each other, trading insults or squabbling, and a neatly-turned plot involving that indispensable item of situation comedy – the missing file. There is plenty of easy laughter, some of it at the expense of the Executive Officer who wears a bowler-hat and carries an umbrella, a figure sufficiently remote and ridiculous to lull the audience into a false sense of security. The music lesson scene also seduces the audience into a mood of relaxed enjoyment, for Major Silva, with his affected accent and ignorance of local musical forms, provides a figure at which almost all can laugh. This appears to be Soyinka at his most comforting, expending his efforts on making elaborate fun of the patently ridiculous. The exchange is strategically placed for it allows the playwright to catch his audience off-guard and strike hard between the eyes with the last scene: the meeting with the rag-bag of religious leaders – aptly described at one point as 'Thieves! Robbers! Rapists and cut-throats!' Laughter at their antics dries up when Jero's plan unfolds; a cold chill of recognition moves along the spine and the hair rises on the back of the neck when he says: 'Let the actuality of power see itself reflected in (our) image, reflected and complemented.' The crooks and charlatans, the thieves, thugs, liars and villains dress themselves in CASA army uniforms and 'reflect and complement' Gowon and his bemedalled cronies. Transformed on the outside by smart, if slightly incongruous, uniforms, they remain as rotten as ever underneath.

Regarded in the light of the ending, the play takes on a very sinister aspect and it becomes clear that there is a deep seriousness in this subversive and pugnacious work. The audience is invited to despise the 'high priests' of Gowon's junta, the 'familiar brigade' with their braided jackets and blood-stained trousers, for it is such 'cheer-leaders of national disaster' who are Soyinka's targets.

The drama provides an obvious and revealing contrast with the earlier 'Jero Play' – and looks forward to the agit-prop sketches of the eighties. As the post-Civil War years demanded, it is far more vicious in its attack and its vision is bleaker than the earlier 'Jero Play'. In *The Trials* there had been determined opposition from Amope, and Jero had, at the end, been extended in coping with Chume: in *Jero's Metamorphosis* there is no challenge from women, indeed Rebecca is completely 'under Jero's spell', and the 'once bitten' Chume is ensnared by Jero's seductive words for a second time. Jero negotiates with prophets and civil servants alike from an apparently invincible position. There are no grounds for hope of positive change in this play, and Soyinka has been charged with fatalism, pessimism and nihilism. In fact, the very writing of the play was an act of self-assertion against the prevailing tyranny and against the brutalisation of Nigeria.

The playwright sent copies of the script to several friends asking them to produce it. There was little response in Nigeria and the world première of *Jero's Metamorphosis* took place (during February 1974) at Bristol with a production directed by Glynne Wickham and mounted by the University's drama department. The play did not receive a widely publicised Nigerian production until it was

mounted at the National Theatre in Lagos during June 1981
– when the soldiers were temporarily in their barracks. The
grounds for pessimism in relation to this play ultimately lie
not in the completeness of Jero's coup, but in the reluctance
of African directors and actors to hold this mirror up to
military regimes. Soyinka's courage and out-spokenness
have not been matched by similar qualities in others.

In response to a commission from the National Theatre
of Great Britain, Soyinka adapted *The Bacchae* by Euripides, a play which had first attracted his attention while he
was an undergraduate at Ibadan. The search for the
meaning of Euripides' *Bacchae* has exercised scholars over
the centuries, but about what happens in a literal sense
there is little disagreement. Soyinka took the bones, and
some of the flesh, of the original and completed it in such a
way tht his own ideas on power, ritual, religion and tragedy
became clear.

The Greek play opens with a speech from Dionysos, son
of Zeus and Semele, who returns with a group of female
devotees to his maternal home, Thebes, to avenge the
suffering and death of his mother. He touches his aunt,
Agave, and other women of Thebes with bacchanalian
frenzy, causing them to abandon their homes for the
mountains. Shortly after the play opens, two old men, the
soothsayer, Tiresias, and Dionysos' grandfather, Kadmos,
enter. They agree that Dionysos is a god and prepare to
worship him, but Pentheus, King of Thebes, son of Agave
and cousin of Dionysos, is enraged. Deaf to the advice of
his seniors, he is determined to challenge Dionysos and
when the god is brought in under guard, the young ruler
rails at him and attempts to lock him up. This attempt fails
completely when Dionysos demonstrates his powers by
moving the earth and by causing men to hallucinate. The
next verbal confrontation between Pentheus and Dionysos

is interrupted by a report concerning the women's strange behaviour on Mount Cithairon. Pentheus intends to respond to their actions with force, but Dionysos, playing on the ruler's curiosity and his supressed femininity, persuades him to dress up as a woman and spy on the Bacchantes. Pentheus exits in feminine attire and, in due course, a messenger reports that he has been discovered by the women and, in the belief that they are dismembering a lion, torn to pieces. Agave enters carrying her son's head, initially unaware that she has killed Pentheus. In Euripides' version this is not the end of Agave's suffering, for in a vindictive speech Dionysos banishes her and Kadmos from Thebes.

Soyinka's undergraduate Greek, eroded by 'a twenty-year rust', was, he says, not good enough to enable him to work from the original text. Instead, like many other adaptors, he used existing translations, and particularly those by Gilbert Murray and William Arrowsmith, as sources. He took a few lines directly from these translations into his text, incorporated passages from his poem 'Idanre' and introduced chants from *oriki* verses in praise of Ogun. These are not self-indulgent or opportunistic interpolations but expressions of the perspective which he brought to the reshaping of the whole text: he built his awareness of the similarities and differences between Ogun and Dionysos into his version of *The Bacchae*.

He also made structual changes which introduced scenes showing the kinship of Dionysos, Hercules and Christ. These, with the parallels with Ogun established by the text, created links between Yoruba religion and major religious traditions which had affected Europe. The version also incorporated ideas related to those expressed in Soyinka's essay on Yoruba tragedy, 'The Fourth Stage', where he argued that Ogun is best understood in Hellenic values as a totality of Dionysian, Apollonian and Promethean virtues. Soyinka's Dionysos is significantly more masculine than the figure found in his sources, more Ogun-like. Where Euripides' Dionysos, in Arrowsmith's translation, has *a soft, even effeminate appearance*, Soyinka's god has a *calm, rugged strength*. The god's opening monologue pays scant attention to desire for revenge and stresses instead his wish to restore or bring life. This restorative quality is present in an unmistakable manner at the end of the Nigerian version.

Soyinka's Pentheus is also distinctive, being associated very strongly with death, repression and megalomania. These links are established visually at the start of the play by a set which includes a row of crucified slaves and then by the abrupt and dictatorial manner which Pentheus adopts. A comparison of the English texts draws attention to the fact that the Pentheus of Euripides, in Murray's and Arrowsmith's translations, does not once use the word 'order' in his opening speech, whereas Soyinka's Pentheus uses that revealing word prominently and repeatedly. Soyinka's Pentheus further betrays his desire to control and dominate at all costs by the brutal way in which he deals with the elderly Tiresias and an Old Slave – a display of violence towards an old man which would be particularly harshly condemned in Yoruba society.

Soyinka's experience of ritual as a living and varied reality made him sensitive to the ritual elements which are apparent from a close study of Euripides' play. *The Bacchae* has, in fact, frequently been cited, by Gilbert Murray and others, as a drama in which the ritual roots of theatre can be apprehended. Soyinka gave prominence to the ritualistic and sacrificial elements, for instance he incorporated a purification rite in which Tiresias offers himself for ritual flagellation.

Soyinka's approach to the text involved reading the work

of Marxist and Marxist-influenced interpreters and his *Bacchae of Euripides* reflects their social and economic analyses. The Slaves' chants reveal Soyinka's interest in Marxist perceptions and show that he can write ideologically oriented and revolutionary verse if he wants to. The play's concern with political revolution was not at odds with its interest in ritual for, as Soyinka argues in 'Drama and the Revolutionary Ideal', revolution can express itself through the metaphor of ritual and transform it. In his version of *The Bacchae of Euripides* he shows this process at work.

Soyinka's most striking alterations to the sources are found towards the end of his play. For the mother's sense of self-inflicted loss and the harsh punishments of Euripides, Soyinka substituted a powerful image of the regenerative power of revolution and of sacrifice – even of unwilling sacrifice. The final tableau is a wine-spouting head, surrounded by wine-swilling celebrants and, as the lights fade, there is a *glow around the heads of Pentheus and Agave*. Soyinka had previously celebrated the power of sacrifice only tentatively. It was a 'fact' he had encountered in the 'ripeness' of rust, in the lush grass growing where animals had been sacrificed and in the new sense of purpose he felt – fleetingly – in some aspects of life in post-Civil War Nigeria. Since the principle of regeneration through a sacrificial death is present in several religions, in many other traditions, and in the literary criticism of Wilson Knight, it cannot be regarded as in any sense unique to Soyinka. But he has made it a distinctive part of his artistic personality; he found it in his culture and realized it memorably in the conclusion to his treatment of the Greek play in which a tyrant's blood fertilizes the field.

The Bacchae of Euripides opened at the Old Vic, then the home of the British National Theatre, on 2 August

1973, with a distinguished cast which included Constance Cummings as Agave, John Shrapnel as Pentheus and Martin Shaw as Dionysos. It was directed by Roland Joffe. The production was well attended, but a number of the critics were hostile and the reaction as a whole was decidedly 'mixed'. The most penetrating of the numerous reviews was by Albert Hunt who brought an awareness of Soyinka's purpose to his analysis of what had gone wrong with the production. He wrote: 'Soyinka has come into direct collision with the unyielding amateurism of the British professional theatre. The company that presents Soyinka's play contains a drummer who can't drum, dancers who can't dance, and actors whose only concept of narrative acting is to begin every speech in the flat clipped tones that used to characterise British war movies, and then to rise in a gradual crescendo towards uncontrolled emotional wallowing. Where the play calls for ecstasy, the girls in the chorus offer a well-bred imitation of a hop at the local disco; and where the play calls for horror, we're given a crude imitation of a Madame Tussaud head, out of which spurts pink paint. The strength of Soyinka's final assertion is frittered away in a grotesque attempt, by this production, to express release'.[1]

Soyinka's adaptation undoubtedly makes great demands on its director and its cast, but it is not an impossible play to put on. Indeed it made a great impact in Kingston, Jamaica, when produced there by Carroll Dawes. It is a very powerful drama in which Soyinka clearly defines himself in relation to a masterpiece of European drama: in it he carves a new image to set beside the mask of tragedy long familiar to European theatre-goers. Unfortunately, but probably inevitably, the sensitivity which prompted the commissioning of *The Bacchae of Euripides* did not extend to the

London production and audiences did not see the new mask clearly.

Death and the King's Horseman, written while Soyinka was at Churchill College, Cambridge, was a play which he had been mulling over since 1960. In that year Ulli Beier, a teacher and writer working in Nigeria, had suggested that certain events which took place at Oyo some fifteen years before would be a suitable basis for an Independence play. In the early seventies, distanced from the maelstrom of Nigerian politics, with limited academic responsibilities, and confronted by prejudiced British attitudes, Soyinka had the leisure and sense of purpose to use the episode in a play. He recognised that the story commented on the qualities required of leaders and on the way the British tended to regard other peoples and other cultures. The play, 'triggered' it seems by a bust of Winston Churchill, was appropriately given a first reading in Cambridge.

The episode which Ulli Beier had suggested was that of the interrupted ritual suicide of the King's Horseman at Oyo in 1945. 'Interrupted ritual' had featured frequently in Soyinka's work over the years, in this instance the interruption not only focussed on a specific historical event, but also provided a general image for colonial intervention. Some details about what happened at Oyo provide a relevant background to the study of the play.

On Tuesday, 19th December 1944, the Alafin of Oyo, Oba Siyenbola Oladigbolu I, died after a reign of thirty-three years. The Master of his Horse, his 'Horseman' – Olokun Esin Jinadu, had enjoyed a privileged position during the Alafin's reign and it seems to have been assumed by the people of Oyo that he would 'follow his master' by commiting suicide, though just how faithfully the custom was observed during the forties is open to debate. On 19

December, Jinadu was delivering a message at the village of Ikoyi near to Oyo. About three weeks later, on 4 January 1945, he returned to Oyo, dressed himself in white and began dancing through the streets towards the house of Bashorun Ladokun, a customary prelude to committing suicide. It was apparently anticipated that he would end his life by the established means of taking poison or allowing a relative to strangle him. However, at this point the British colonial officer in authority at Oyo intervened: he sent an order to the Bashorun's house that Jinadu should be apprehended and taken to the Residency. This order was carried out and Jinadu was taken into custody. When word of the arrest spread, Jinadu's youngest son, Murana, killed himself in his father's place.[2]

Soyinka describes his play as 'based on' these events but it is difficult to determine how well informed he was about the details. In all probability he knew only the bare bones of the episode. Some of the alterations, such as the setting of the confrontation during the Second World War and the introduction of a visit by the Prince of Wales to Nigeria, were made for what may be called, following Soyinka's 'Author's Note', 'minor reasons of dramaturgy'. Others may be the result of ignorance, or misinformation. The dating of the event in 1946 in the 'Author's Note', for instance, is an inaccuracy which serves no purpose.

Soyinka's play opens in the market-place where the King's Horseman, 'Elesin Oba', *a man of enormous vitality, speaks, dances and sings with . . . infectious enjoyment.* Accompanied by his drummers and Praise Singer, Elesin Oba is following his dead lord, he is on his way to commit suicide. It transpires that Elesin has not cast off the delight he has long taken in worldly pleasures: he checks his progress between the market stalls and encourages the market women to deck him in rich cloth. Then he sees and desires a beautiful young woman, the Bride, and dallies for a second time. The leader of the market-women, Iyaloja, whose son is bethrothed to the Bride, briefly tries to dissuade him, but Elesin Oba is determined to 'let/Seed that will not serve the stomach/On the way remain behind.' Iyaloja, unwilling to 'blight the day when all should be openness and light', bids the women prepare the young woman. The first act closes as the bedecked Bride is presented to the glowing Elesin, and Iyaloja's words of warning ring in the ears of the audience.

The second act is set on the verandah of the house of the town's District Officer, Simon Pilkings in Soyinka's drama – an appropriate name for the brisk subordinate of limited intellectual capacity that Soyinka has created. Pilkings and his wife, Jane, are dressed up in the clothes they intend to wear to a fancy-dress ball at the Residency – *egungun* masquerade costumes – and are dancing a tango. The image is grotesque, and immediately reveals the attitude of the couple towards the community in which they live and over which Pilkings has, thanks to the soldiers at his command, considerable power. Serjeant Amusa clumsily interrupts the dance with important news, which he is reluctant to reveal while Pilkings is dressed as a cult figure. Although a Muslim, Amusa has enough respect for the masquerade costume to refuse to 'talk against death to person in uniform of death.' Eventually he writes out his report and we learn that 'Elesin Oba is to commit death tonight as a result of native custom.' Simon and Jane Pilkings construe this to mean that a ritual murder is about to take place and call on their servant Joseph for confirmation. Joseph, a Christian convert, explains that Elesin Oba 'will not kill anybody and no one will kill him. He will simply die.' From the ensuing conversation Simon Pilkings' lack of respect for Christianity becomes apparent and the audience learns of his previous intervention in the life of the Elesin's family: four years earlier he had helped Olunde, Elesin's son, to get to medical school in England. The District Officer sends a note to Amusa ordering him to arrest Elesin Oba and the act closes with more Latin American rhythms and with Jane's excitement at the news that the Prince of Wales will attend the ball.

For the third act, the scene shifts back to the market where the women are protecting Elesin's marriage bower from Amusa's forces. The women halt the policemen's progress by teasing them and questioning their virility. The humour provides a ribald background to the consummation of the marriage and further explores the theme of man-hood. The success of the market-women, and then Iyaloja, in halting the police is followed by the triumph of their daughters in a charade which ridicules the white commun-ity's affected and trivial pre-occupations. Amusa is made to look foolish and forced to retreat, but he leaves, threaten-ing to return. Elesin then enters bearing the cloth which testifies that his Bride was a virgin. As a dirge wells up and the lights fade, he moves into a deep trance, resuming his interrupted movement towards the transitional gulf, which, in the cosmology of the play, separates the living from the dead.

The setting for act four is the Great Hall of the Residency, *redolent*, the stage-direction reads, *of the tawdry decadence of a far-flung but key imperial frontier*. Couples are dancing in fancy-dress and the Prince of Wales enters to the strains of 'Rule Britannia' execrably played by the police band. A waltz follows and then, as the 'ritual' of introductions begins, Simon and Jane Pilkings delight the assembled company by showing off their costumes and imitating the mock-threatening behaviour of *egungun* masqueraders. A sinister note is sounded during this sequence since it becomes apparent that the *tawdry deca-dence* of the decor extends to the imperial officers who trivialise all they do not understand and are united by an utter contempt for the community in which they work. Pilkings is called apart – *his* dance interrupted for a second time – when Amusa arrives. Since it is clear that trouble is brewing in the town, the DO goes off to change out of one 'uniform of death' into another, and to take action. Left behind, Jane is approached by a young Nigerian in a sober suit; he turns out to be Olunde, who has returned 'on the mail-boat' after hearing of the Alafin's death and in anticipation of the consequences for his father. The conversation which follows covers British attitudes, war, deeds of honour, Olunde's experiences and the events which are taking place in the town. The young man assumes that his father has committed suicide, and, by way of explanation, says: 'His will power has always been enor-mous.' The pace of events quickens as Olunde is first abused by a bigoted colonial officer and then reveals his moral and intellectual superiority. A bellow of rage from off-stage anticipates the entrance of Elesin in hand cuffs. Surprised and dismayed Olunde rejects his father with the words 'I have no father, eater of left-overs', and walks slowly away leaving the light fading on the sobbing horseman who has failed his master, his son, his people and himself.

When the final act opens, relationships are clarified by a highly symbolic setting: a prison in which slaves were once held prior to being sent to the coast. Elesin is a prisoner; Pilkings is in his policeman's uniform. They talk about the events of the day, honour, duty, and society, speaking to each other through *a wide iron-barred gate*, which impris-ons Elesin and symbolises the barriers to understanding between the two men. In this conversation, Elesin reveals a depth of understanding which repeatedly exposes the shallowness of the Englishman.

The two men are joined by Jane and then by Iyaloja, who upraids Elesin for the way he has betrayed his community. Her eloquent denunciation includes the following summary:

> We fed you sweetmeats such as we hoped awaited you on the other side. But you said No, I must eat the world's left-overs. (*Six Plays* p. 210)

Elesin tries to justify himself with a speech which puts the blame on outsiders:

> It is when the alien hand pollutes the source of will, when a stranger force of violence shatters the mind's calm resolution, this is when a man is made to commit the awful treachery of relief, commit in his thought the unspeakable blasphemy of seeing the hand of the gods in the alien rupture of his world. (*Six Plays* pp. 211-212)

Iyaloja brushes aside this explanation, and the fact that the play has presented Elesin's wilful dallying in the market but not his arrest by Amusa's men reinforces the impression that he is thrashing around for some way of justifying himself rather than genuinely searching his soul.

Iyaloja then announces the approach of 'a burden'. When it is carried in, to the accompaniment of a dirge, the Praise Singer confronts Elesin, exploring still further his failure of will, asking why Elesin had not enlisted assistance in committing suicide, and retracing, in expressive and reverberating imagery, the course which Elesin had taken. When the covering of the burden is removed, Olunde's body is revealed and, with the chains which secure his wrists, Elesin strangles himself. In one final, clumsy intervention, the last of a series, Pilkings moves forward to close Elesin's eyes, but Iyaloja, here as so often a figure of true authority, cries 'Let him alone'. She summons the Bride to perform this last service and to scatter a little earth on Elesin's eye lids. A dirge rises as the lights fade on the tableau of corpses and swaying women.

By imaginative handling of historical material and subtle stage craft, Soyinka created a compelling and substantial drama. The amendments to the sources and the innovations he made allowed him to bring into focus several themes. For instance, the introduction of the Bride enabled him to present Elesin's attachment to the pleasures of the flesh. The introduction of the Prince and the setting of the drama in war-time made it possible for him to contrast two codes of honour, both embodied in the summons to fulfill responsibilities and obey patterns of inheritance: codes apparent in the privileges and obligations imposed on Elesin, and in the courage which carried the Prince of Wales across the 'Nazi-infested seas'. By making Olunde a medical student with first-hand experience of the carnage of the Second World War, Soyinka was able to contrast the savage blood-letting of Europe with the strictly controlled sacrifices of Yorubaland.

The characterisation and the stagecraft of the play contribute to a moving and coherent examination of the colonial encounter in which the arrogant, supercillious and well-armed British confronted a social structure and a metaphysical system they did not begin to understand, did not even try to appreciate. However, Soyinka is only partly concerned to make the British appear insensitive and ridiculous, a major concern is to present the Yoruba world and world-view on stage – and in this he is also successful.

In his 'Author's Note', Soyinka cautioned the would-be

producer of *Horseman* against what he described as the 'sadly familiar reductionist tendency' of regarding the play as about the 'clash of cultures'. He invited directors to elicit 'the play's threnodic essence'. The 'note', which I suspect was written some time after the play, reflected the feeling that the arrogant and myopic vision of Pilkings was not a summation of British or European culture but a distortion of it. Ultimately Pilkings is hardly more capable of representing western civilisation than Lakunle and, in Soyinka's view, there can be no clash of cultures when only one culture, Yoruba culture in this case, is presented in in depth. The 'Note' draws attention to the metaphysical dimension of the play, and this element is clearly present in the carefully contrasted representatives of religion, and irreligion. Christians and Muslims are there, as well as Simon Pilkings, who has no respect for any religion, and *orisha* worshippers. In the course of the play Elesin approaches 'the gulf of transition' and, though he stumbles, he suggests something of the passage in image and dance. In fact, he has certain qualities in common with Ogun, the first to cross the abyss and Soyinka's ideal tragic protagonist, but it is, of course, Olunde who proves himself the true devotee of the God of Iron. It is easy to get laughs at the expense of the fancy dressers in the Residency, not so easy to bring out the metaphysical contrasts and developments. The importance of holding on to the second is, I suggest, the import of the 'Author's Note'.

The form of the play contains little that surprises a reader or an audience familiar with the European theatrical tradition. Indeed, attention has been drawn to the 'five-act structure' and to the 'Shakespearian' quality of the play. Shakespeare was certainly present in the playwright's creative sub conscious in Cambridge, particularly the

Shakespeare who wrote about 'bright honour' in *Henry IV* and about suicide in the last scene of *Antony and Cleopatra*, which Wilson Knight analysed so tellingly in terms of dissolving into death and which Soyinka referred to with admiration in his talk on 'Shakespeare and the Living Dramatist'. There is also in Soyinka's play a concern with ritual: both the trivial rituals of the Prince's progress, such as the playing of 'Rule Britannia' and the presentation of selected couples, and also the far more intense and meaningful ritual of the procession of the Horseman.

As in his version of *The Bacchae*, Soyinka exploited areas of cultural overlap between Europe and Africa: he had also emphasied characteristic qualities of the African tradition. In the tableau which closes *Horseman*, the living surround two dead bodies, but the dead are not simply being mourned, as they might be in parts of the Western tradition and as they are in the last acts of some European plays. Olunde has triumphed in death, through embracing death he has salvaged some honour for his family and his death is a cause for rejoicing. His achievement is all the greater because he died despite the opportunity of escape provided by Pilkings: he was, in a sense, responding to the call of 'his blood', he was also, like protagonists in earlier plays by Soyinka, making a voluntary sacrifice. It is in this context that the name Soyinka selected for the Horseman's son becomes significant, for, according to Dan Izevbaye, 'Olunde' may be a contracted form of 'Olundande' (One who liberates) or of 'Olundanide' (He who rises by himself), the second alternative would then mean 'honour restored' or 'honour arisen'.[3] The mixture of emotions which should be felt as the lights fade on the tableau is distinctive, a mingling of sadness and joy. In this rich masterpiece of expressive poetry, strong characterisation, subtle theatrical technique and sinuous argument, Soyinka has, once again, extended the range of drama and challenged audiences to respond to a new experience. He has created a different sort of tragedy.

Soyinka has directed the play twice, once in Ife (1976), once in Chicago (1979). The reactions to the productions, chilly in Ife, very enthusiastic in Chicago, underline the point that *Horseman* is a play of the Cambridge Period. It is part of a dialogue with Europe – and, by extension, with America – rather than a direct contribution to the debates raging in Nigeria. This is not to say the play is irrelevant to Nigeria, it has, in fact, much to reveal to that country about leadership, responsibility, honour and self-sacrifice, much that is relevant and that should be listened to.

Ironically, part of the reason for the cool reception by critics in Ife was one reason for its huge success in America: the use of a feudal court as an image through which themes could be explored. For many Nigerians, suffering from the social upheavals caused by a civil war and an oil-boom, the trappings of majesty, the King's this and the King's that, created a block to the reception of the play's vision. For many Americans, particularly Afro-Americans, this same courtly Africa was one to which they were very eager to respond. As the years pass, the play will speak increasingly to Nigerians and will retain its attractions for those who come to it from the European, American or Afro-American traditions. Its qualities will be more fully appreciated.

During this century, exile has provided stimulation for many writers and artists. From the years 1971 to 1975, Soyinka's second exile, came three important plays, each illustrating in one way or another the characteristics of exile: the determination to contribute to developments in the homeland while carrying forward a debate with the culture in which the exile is spent. The combination of influences provoked, in *Death and the King's Horseman*, a major contribution to twentieth century drama.

8
Plays for Nigeria of the Seventies and Eighties

After his return to Nigeria in 1975, Soyinka became increasingly concerned with the need to communicate political ideas to a mass audience through the performing arts. He developed a distinctive agit-prop theatre which made particularly effective use of music and song. During this period, he wrote *Opera Wonyosi* (1977), *Before the Blow-out* (made up of *Home to Roost* and *Big Game Safari* (1978)); *Rice Unlimited* (1981), *Die Still Rev. Dr Godspeak!* (1982) – a commissioned radio play which emerged as the stage play *Requiem for a Futurologist* (1983), and *Priority Projects* (made up of *Festac 77*, *Green Revolution*, *Ethical Revolution* and *Abuja*, 1983). In addition to these works, he also drafted *A Play of Giants*, scheduled for performance at the University of Yale during 1981 but not produced or published until 1984.

A certain proportion of this work has not been published

and was, by its nature, ephemeral, 'hit and run' drama which may never be available to a reading public. The period also produced a series of political songs, such as those which formed part of *Priority Projects*, and appeared on a record with 'Unlimited Liability Company', and 'Take the First Step'.

Soyinka sought a framework for his satirical bombardment on the numerous vices of oil-boom Nigeria, and found it in Bertolt Brecht's early masterpiece *The Threepenny Opera* (1928), itself an adaptation of John Gay's *The Beggar's Opera* (1728). John Willett has provided a brisk summary of Brecht's version: 'The outline is Gay's: Macheath secretly marries Polly, daughter of his fellow-crook Peachum. Peachum plans his arrest; he flees, but is caught through the treachery of Jenny and her co-whores. In gaol he finds another old love, Lucy, who helps him to escape. He is recaptured with yet another woman, taken to be executed, and reprieved in a deliberately artificial happy ending.' Willett continued: 'about nine-tenths of the dialogue has been re-written. Innovations include the second scene (the stable wedding), the character of Tiger Brown (*vice* Gay's Lockit), and Peachum's whole business of organizing and fitting out beggars.'[1] Soyinka generally followed Brecht and he included the innovations introduced into the German version. He also created new characters and added new sequences, thereby radically transforming his sources and giving *Opera Wonyosi* a distinctively African and Nigerian flavour.

An indication of his approach to his sources and his satirical attack is provided by his handling of the coronation. It was important for the Gay-Brecht originals that there was a major state function going on in the background to the play. Gay, writing in and about England, had made this a coronation and Brecht, who retained the English setting for his version, kept it. Soyinka wanted to locate his adaptation in Africa, and, in a list of 'acknowledgements and disclaimers', he expressed 'his indebtedness to His Imperial Diminutive Emperor Bokassa I of Central Africa, who solved the geographical dilemma of this opera by taking a timely stride backward into pre-history, and being crowned.' Bokassa's coronation was, incidentally, Neo-Napoleonic in its magnificence: it involved a two-tonne throne of gilt bronze, a 124-carat diamond crown, an ermine-fringed robe and over 2,000 foreign guests. It provided not only a plot device but an image of decadence which deserved to be attacked in its own right as an outrage to Africa, a symptom of vulgar opulence which was 'reflected and complemented' by many of the play's first audience. Jean-Bedel Bokassa was overthrown after his involvement in killing school children was revealed. This qualified him for inclusion in *Opera Wonyosi* where he has a scene in which to reveal his propensities. Such changes in points of reference, tones, musical sources, and character have the effect of making this version of Gay/Brecht an intensely Soyinkan piece of theatre.

A roll-call of the injustice, anti-social behaviour, arrogance, corruption, and profligacy pilloried or attacked in the play would be an itemisation of the abuses in Nigeria during the mid-seventies. There are references, for instance, to the Igbeti Marble Affair which involved several unexplained deaths; the Cement Scandal in which fortunes were made and workmen suffered; the frequent resort to violence by the police; the destruction of Fela Anikulapo-Kuti's 'Kalakuta Republic' by Nigerian soldiers; the bland verdict of the Commission of Enquiry into that affair; the public execution of armed robbers in a carnival atmosphere at Bar Beach; the dilatory attitude of metropolitan and highway authorities which allowed corpses to decompose by the road sides, and the servility of lecturers who lobbied, or begged, for promotion. The list of precise targets is extensive, and if an 'Annotated Edition' of Soyinka's Collected Works is published they will all be described in the foot-notes. For the present purpose, Soyinka's preface to the rehearsal script provides the best indication of the mood and the times in which he wrote *Opera Wonyosi* and, in 1977, directed it:

> The post Civil-War period after an initial period of uncertainty – two or three years at the most – has witnessed Nigeria's self-engorgement at the banquet of highway robberies, public executions, public floggings and other institutionalised sadisms, arsons, individual and mass megalomania, racketeering, hoarding, epidemic road-abuse and reckless slaughter, exhibition-ism – private and institutional – callous and contemp-tuous ostentation, casual cruelties, wanton destruction, slummification, Nairamania, and its attendant atavism (ritual murder for wealth), an orgy of physical filth, champagne, usuary, gadgetry, blood . . . the near-total collapse of human communication . . .

Some of the satire in *Opera Wonyosi* strikes home through the characters. This is most clearly the case with the portrait of Bokassa, 'Boky', in which Soyinka employs his highly developed skill for caricature and parody to create a tyrant who is seen to be confused and ridiculous as well as horrifying, a man whose jumbled words and twisted ideas reveal the monstrous tangle of his mind. As usual in Soyinka's plays there is an abundance of sharply differenti-ated and crisply realised characters, several of them given depth by being, to some extent, representative figures. Beside Anikura, the Peachum of the sources, to whom

Soyinka has given the name of a notorious Nigerian criminal, and De Madam (Mrs Peachum) stand their crew of henchmen and beggars which includes Professor Bamgbapo, a time-serving academic on sabbatical, A.G. Alatako, lawyer extraordinary, and a new recruit, Ahmed. Macheath's band of thugs is deliberately coarser; it includes Matar, Baba Hadji, Dan Dare and Hookfinger Jake. Between the two camps hovers a fortune-seeking prophet, Brother Jerubabel - or 'Jeru' for short. In a note to the programme for the first production, Soyinka affirmed that, aside from Bokassa, 'the genius of race portrayed in this opera is entirely, indisputably and vibrantly Nigerian.'

Other satirical targets are hit by the movement of the narrative. Soyinka exploits to the full the subversive comment contained in the fitting-out of Ahmed as a beggar, a sequence which reveals that everyone is 'begging for a slice of the action' and that exploiting the tender-hearted is truly a science. Another 'metamorphosis', that of Macheath from highwayman/armed robber to legitimate businessman, is not original – many 'Godfathers' have 'gone legit' – but it is handled with precision and presented with convincing detail in Soyinka's version. The episode in which lawyer Alatako 'proves' by ruthless logic that the army is a secret society demonstrates yet another of Soyinka's many talents as a satirist, the ability to reduce apparent sense to patent absurdity.

Although the musical element is not entirely satisfactory, some of the play's most telling criticism is made through the songs. Soyinka was particularly eclectic in his musical sources: his version opens, as does Brecht's, with 'Mack the Knife', for which Soyinka wrote pungent new verses; later on it employs another Kurt Weil score, that for 'The Song of Jenny Leveller'. Elsewhere he draws on music by Donald Swann ('Blood, Blood, Glorious Blood'), nursery tunes ('Who Killed Nio Niga'), Israel Ijemanze ('The Song of ngh – ngh – ngh'), and 'The St Louis Blues' ('The Song of Lost Innocence'). Although the lyrics cut through to make telling comments, the score is a musical mish-mash, and even Soyinka's presence as conductor during the Ife run of *Opera Wonyosi* could not give it a coherent style.

The Ife production, which Soyinka directed with Yemi Ogunbigi as his assistant, set out to disturb and challenge its audiences in ways that the printed text does not always convey. A characteristic note is struck by the first speech of the play: a Disc Jockey's introduction which begins in an apparently off-hand manner with 'I'll just introduce myself.' These words are a deliberate attempt to sow doubt in the minds of members of the audience about the status of what is being presented. Is it a formal piece of theatre in which actors recite lines they have learned and go through movements they have rehearsed? Or, is it 'an event', 'a happening', at which almost anything may take place? For the most part the production was the former, and even when the actors moved off the stage and into the auditorium they did so in a rehearsed manner. The 'rehearsed' quality may not have been apparent to members of the first audience when the Attack Traders, a multitude of Mother Courages who crossed and re-crossed the no-man's land between opposing forces during the Civil War, stripped the valuables from 'corpses' on stage and erupted, like belligerent ice-cream sales-girls, to hawk their gruesome wares among the audience. This eruption was, in fact, rehearsed, but there were also occasions when the director instructed that unrehearsed sequences should be performed. For instance, on the opening night, and after consulting only those directly involved, Soyinka, as conductor, summoned Colonel Moses (Brecht's Tiger Brown) on stage to belabour the erring Professor Bamgbapo. The move was so unexpected and the performances by Femi Euba (Moses) and Biodun Jeyifo (Bamgbapo) so convincing that even members of the cast thought that a real 'military assault' was taking place. The levels of reality were particularly hard to penetrate because Euba was unrecognisable to many of the cast in his authentic uniform and because Jeyifo was politically radical in real life and a target for attacks by reactionary forces. This episode challenged members of the audience to observe the reflection of the truth in the fiction they were watching; it forced them to come to terms with a particular image of what was happening in their University.

The procession with the coffin, which is described in the published version of the play, was not part of the rehearsal text. The sequence was introduced in mid-run following a newspaper report to the effect that the columnist and social reformer Tai Solarin, with a group of friends, had collected a much publicised corpse which had been decomposing in a Lagos street and delivered it to the offices of the Lagos Town Council. Soyinka got his cast to reproduce Solarin's procession, which was both a public spirited act and a political gesture. In the context of Soyinka's production, it would have been perfectly understandable if members of the audience had been shaken by the pall-bearers and had wondered whether Soyinka was delivering a corpse from the Ibadan-Ife road to the audience in Oduduwa Hall. He is bold enough to have done so, there would have been corpses available and he had directed *Opera Wonyosi* in such a way as to create a constant air of uncertainty in the auditorium: it could have been a corpse-filled coffin. Soyinka challenged the expectations of his audiences, jolted them out of their complacency, confronted them with the realities of their situations.

The world première of *Opera Wonyosi* took place on the

night of the University of Ife's Convocation (16 December), before an audience which contained many official guests and several national figures. Soyinka has indicated that the effect on these people was considerable, particularly on a military governor and on some security officers. The efforts (their efforts?), successful as it turned out, to prevent the production being seen in Lagos further indicate the effectiveness of the satiricial attacks. The official response, like that of Sir Robert Walpole when confronted with Gay's stage image of himself, was to 'grin and bear it' while the performance lasted and then ensure that the opera was not mounted again. The proof of the power of Soyinka's production was that it was confined to Ife.

Leftist critics have been only a little kinder to *Opera Wonyosi* than the establishment. Reviewers, including the actor-academic-activist Jeyifo, complained that the musical stressed the negative elements in the society, neglected the growth points and was flawed by lacking a 'solid class-perspective'.[2] In his 'Foreword' to the published text, Soyinka responded to these critics and attacked 'the mouthers and opportunists among the African neo-Marxists'. He defined the writer's role as being 'merely complementary to that of the politician, sociologist, technocrat, worker, ideologue, priest, student, teacher etc., not one which can usurp one or all of these roles in entirety without forfeiting its own claim to a distinctive vocation.' Soyinka balanced the need to reflect the 'positive points' with the necessity to 'expose, reflect, indeed magnify the decadent, rotted underbelly of a society that has lost its direction, jettisoned all sense of values and is careering down a precipice as fast as the latest artificial boom can take it.' This deeply-felt statement is a justification for much of his work during the late seventies and the eighties.

Opera Wonyosi has found a place among Soyinka's

published texts, but it is not likely, given its undistinguished score and the topicality of its satire, that it will be revived. Indeed it is certain that Soyinka would not want it to be revived in a reverential manner. Its value is as an example of how suitable European models can be used to speak to particular audiences about particular problems. It stands as a model of adaptation ready to be adapted for changing circumstances.

For Soyinka's own development the work's lasting influence was in terms of character and music. Peachum and his colleagues were partly responsible for inspiring Anikura and his cronies who came to life in the plot of *Opera Wonyosi* and later enjoyed a further existence in *Before the Blow-out*. In preparing lyrics and selecting musical styles, Soyinka was stimulated by Brecht's spare language and Weil's harsh score. In the work of Israel Ijemanze he found a local and more lasting influence, a Nigerian musician who could provide a model for his own work in the years ahead. At the end of *Opera Wonyosi*, Anikura sings:

> Who really accumulates and exercises
> Power over others. The currency of that power
> Though it forms the bone of contention
> Soon proves secondary. I tell you –
> Power is delicious . . . Heel! (*Opera Wonyosi*, in Soyinka, *Six Plays*, p. 404)

Having been prevented from appearing in *Opera Wonyosi* in Lagos, Anikura, now styled 'Chief Theophilus Ajijebolorita Onikura' but the same except for the initial letter of his last name, re-emerged in two sketches written for the Guerrilla Theatre Unit of the University of Ife: *Home to Roost* and *Big Game Safari*, known together as

Before the Blow-out. Some of the humour in the sketches is of the same kind as is found in *Wonyosi*, but the texts employ visual effects which enable them to have a certain impact in the lorry-parks and market-places of Nigeria. Unlike *Wonyosi*, the sketches could be easily transported and could be performed almost anywhere.

Home to Roost takes as its subject the activities which followed the lifting of the ban on political activities in Nigeria. During 1978, many politicans, both old and new, began to form parties and woo the media in preparation for their invitation to the electorate to vote for them during 1979. Soyinka's sketch suggests that he did not regard the return or emergence of some of these people as a blessing.

The play is set on an airport runway where Onikura and his henchmen are waiting on a flight of steps to make sure that their descent onto Nigerian soil is caught by the cameras of the press corps. Onikura's entourage includes some of the most vivid characters from *Opera Wonyosi*: including Professor Bamgbapo, Colonel Moses, and Brother Jeru – the opportunist prophet who says his prayers facing 'Jekka', a holy city conveniently placed mid-way between Mecca and Jerusalem. The aircraft is imagined, the steps are real: they improve the audience's sight-lines and provide a focus for attention. When the 'Opening Theme Song' is sung, ears as well as eyes are prepared for the satirical exchanges which follow as Onikura 'meets the press' and gives some of the reasons for his coming 'home to roost'.

The static quality of the work – apart from 'the arrival' nothing much actually happens – and its heavy reliance on verbal humour limit the impact of *Home to Roost* as agit-prop theatre. For instance, only those with an extensive English vocabulary can appreciate the deception involved in the distribution at the airport of printed copies of Onikura's '*spontaneous* homecoming peroration' and can savour the differences between 'ecology' and 'biology', 'consistent' and 'constituent', 'baston' and 'bastion' – all of which are confused by characters in the play. Some of the verbal humour is, however, very broad and would be widely appreciated in Nigeria. For instance, Onikura is one of those who seeks to make an impact by his use of impressive-sounding English words. He booms: 'My friend, I am an institution. When an irresistible force comes to encounter an immovable force, the clash of the irresistible momentum and the immovable mass must result in the atomisation of the lesser in durability of experience and longevity.' The point about this is not whether it makes sense or whether everyone in the audience knows the meaning of every word. The satirist simply wants the listeners to recognise the speech as containing the kind of inflated rhetoric used by certain political 'heavyweights', such as the resilient K.O. Mbadiwe (who had been pilloried in 'Press Conference', a sketch from the sixties). The context establishes Onikura as a coward, a hypocrite and a political opportunist: this sketch discredits all those who 'blow grammar' as he does.

Visual clues are also used to erode credibility. The returning politicians are cowards whose knees shake so uncontrollably on arrival in Nigeria that they make the steps on which they stand vibrate violently and visibly. When Onikura and his wife kiss Nigerian soil, the gesture is supposed to indicate their delight at being home, but because the audience watches both the prelude and the epilogue to this rash gesture it recognises the real feelings of the couple. Nigerian soil revolts them, indeed, it seems, no one at all concerned about health would be so rash as to kiss it! I saw the short play performed during November 1978; it was highly topical and much appreciated by an audience in

Oduduwa Hall at the University of Ife. I do not think that it would have much impact in the streets of Ile-Ife, where it was also presented.

The next episode in the saga of Onikura's bid for political power took its title from that of 'the first film to be made in Africa', *Big Game Safari*. The sketch was triggered by a wave of car thefts which swept Nigeria; for instance a hundred cars were stolen in Ibadan over a thirty day period around September 1978. Soyinka related this sort of news item to the political developments taking place in the country, and suggested, in *Big Game Safari*, that unscrupulous politicians might be responsible. They, after all, needed to secure means of transport in preparation for the election campaign.

Big Game Safari is set in a forest clearing and the essential 'set' consists of a brand-new Igala car, a model produced by Volkswagen, concealed behind a bush, and a lorry. The drama begins, in a manner guaranteed to attract and intrigue a street audience, with Onikura's squad of supporters being drilled by Colonel Moses. The 'troops' are then issued with objects which look like 'futuristic watering-cans' and which are, it transpires, 'metal detectors'. While Moses tries to drill and train his men, Onikura and his wife, Cecilia, argue about ball-room dancing steps: open telemacs, half-hesitations, quick-steps, tango and such like. This argument, which is conducted with elegant demonstrations, attracts the attention of the 'troops' – much to Colonel Moses' disapproval. Eventually, after comments on car thefts, hoarding, and the military regime's 'low profile' policy, the 'troops' scatter and begin to search the 'area'. As the weird metal detectors start flashing, a fearsomely armed watchman springs from a bush. Three of Onikura's men tremble before his arrow, knife and teeth until Moses enters and disarms him. Moses

139

clears away the bush and discovers 'a herd of fifty Igala cars', a cache which will put Onikura's election campaign, literally, 'on the road'.

This is popular, spectacular theatre which exposes the machinations of political leaders; a distinctive, amusing, Soyinkan, form of the Living Newspaper tradition. But Soyinka still had some way to go before he could be said to have fashioned an effective means of reaching and communicating with a mass audience.

The next play to be announced was *A Play of Giants*, but the next dramatic piece to be staged was a very brief, very hastily put together sketch. *Rice Unlimited* addressed itself to the numerous scandals surrounding the importation and distribution of rice. Unfortunately the sketch was ephemeral, and although seen by many people in the centre of Lagos, the performance passed unreviewed and largely unrecorded.

During the seventies, ordinary Nigerians came to regard rice as one of their staple foods. After Shehu Shagari came to power in 1978, millions of naira changed hands overnight through the sale and re-sale of licences to import rice. Trading in rice was also remunerative and bags which were unloaded at Apapa for 38 naira each were sold in the markets for 100 naira and more. In Nigeria during 1981 the price of rice was capable of causing an uprising – it was an explosive issue.

Soyinka's play on the subject was presented by the Guerrilla Theatre Unit in the grounds of the National Museum, near to the centre of Lagos. It was straightforward, simple and repetitive, and after the performance, but in a sense as an extension of it into a more conventional demonstration, the actors piled sacks marked 'rice' in front of the House of Assembly. Then, waving placards inscribed with slogans drawing attention to the inequalities in

Nigerian life, they made their escape by foot and bus before the police could take action. Since a large crowd had gathered to watch the performance and traffic was brought to a standstill around the Museum, the play – as a demonstration at least – can be said to have achieved a certain degree of success. The directness and simplicity of the language used in *Rice Unlimited* and the visual quality of the demonstration marked a new level of achievement for Soyinka as a political dramatist.

The direction of Soyinka's development has frequently been affected by the opportunities available to him and 1982 was no exception. In that year, he responded to an invitation to write a play for the BBC and prepared a script which grew from a prank played by the satirist Jonathan Swift (1667–1754) and from Soyinka's concern about the influence of 'metaphysicians and parapsychologists' on Nigerian life. The play out-grew the half-hour radio format, and, although the radio version, *Die Still, Rev. Dr Godspeak!*, exists, I consider the stage version, *Requiem For a Futurologist* – published 1984, to be the significant text.

Swift embarrassed the astrologer and almanc-maker John Partridge through *The Bickerstaff Letters*. Briefly, the Dean first 'predicted' Partridge's death and then announced it; such was his influence and the cunning of his pen that the poor Partridge was hard put to it to convince people that he was still alive. There were many Partridges in Nigeria during the late seventies and early eighties, the most prominent being 'Dr' Godspower Oyewole, who was regarded by some as a 'world-renowned' metaphysician and parapsychologist. His predictions were widely reported and were taken seriously by millions of people. In addition to exposing the Oyewoles of this world to ridicule, Soyinka wanted to hold up for critical examination the

wording of obituary notices and the extravagence connected with funerals, indeed the manner in which Nigerian
funerals had become occasions for the living to display their
wealth.

The central conflict in *Requiem*, which reveals few debts
to the details of Swift's joke, is between an astrologer, the
Right Rev. Dr Godspeak Igbehodan, and his rival, Brother
Eleazar Hosannah, who has predicted and announced his
death. The play begins with Godspeak besieged in his
house by a crowd determined to believe he is dead, and
takes us through Godspeak's attempts to make contact with
someone, almost anyone, who will, despite Eleazar's
predictions, the obituary notices, the posters which have
appeared and the BBC's report of his death, believe that he
is alive.

As this suggests, there is not much of what is generally
regarded as plot in *Requiem for a Futurologist*, the trap has
been set and the mouse has been caught before the play
opens. All we do is watch the doomed creature's desperate
attempts to escape and wonder how it will meet its end.
This is essentially a dilemma story and a series of encounters, for which precedents can be found in Yoruba folk
tradition. It is also a drama which continues, in a grimly
humourous mode, Soyinka's examination of death.

One of Godspeak's visitors is Kilanko of Upbeat Cutters
and Fitters. From him we gather that the funeral suit which
has been mysteriously ordered for Godspeak is of the very
best, imported and, in view of the Government's 'Low
Profile' policy, banned cloth. The most interesting visitor is
undoubtedly Dr. Semuwe, a fascinating addition to the
extraordinary array of eccentrics Soyinka has created over
the years. He is an unorthodox medical doctor who has
developed his own highly personal perspective on events, a
perspective which he considers an 'unassailable philoso-

phy': his arguments are ingenious and his questions prob-
ing. Although eccentric and idiosyncratic, even he has a
representative dimension, being based on a familiar stage-
type, the comic doctor. Surgery scenes such as he is
involved in are frequently incorporated into school enter-
tainments and comic theatre performances in Nigeria as
elsewhere, and Soyinka is partly re-working a sure-fire
sequence when he has Semuwe test Godspeak's physical
reflexes. But the medical examination sequence, whatever
its independent comic merits, is neatly incorporated within
the total drama. The same point can be made about the
bizarre dialogue between Semuwe and Godspeak which is
amusing in itself, but also focuses the play's concern with
existence and the means of proving that one exists, a
philosophical debate which Soyinka contributed to in
Myth, Literature and the African World.

Semuwe is contrasted, and the shift of mood is deliberate
and obvious, with Nana Okoromfo Dopevi, a master-
carpenter from Kumasi, Ghana, who has been commissioned to make Godspeak's coffin. Dopevi, like many of his
fellow countrymen during the eighties, migrated to Nigeria
following the collapse of the Ghanaian economy and in
pursuit of extravagent and decadent customers. The special
quality of Dopevi's work is that each coffin is custom-made
to a design that is appropriate to the corpse it will contain.
In this instance, he has constructed a coffin shaped like
Godspeak's 'trade-mark': a bowler hat. Soyinka makes a
rather elaborate visual joke here, knowing that his audiences will respond to it.

The pace, which is generally sedate, speeds up a little
towards the end as the parapsychologist, in desperation,
tries to turn the tables on his persecutor by announcing that
Eleazar has been killed in a motor-accident. This fails to
impress the waiting crowd, which, while showing many

characteristics of being a mindless mob, can, it thinks, tell a dead man clutching at straws when it sees one. Godspeak contemplates striking his rival and supplanter down, maintaining stubbornly and with the attractive, grim logic that emerges periodically in the play, 'They can't hang a dead man'. However, he is persuaded by Semuwe to feign death, and the script ends as photographs are taken of Eleazar gazing sadly down at the Right Rev. Dr Godspeak Igbehodan, parapsychologist, deceased – perhaps.

This, at least, is what happens in the rehearsal script. In the 1983 production, which was toured widely in Nigeria, Soyinka took considerable liberties with what he had written. For instance, he opened the play with processions of political parties and the adherents of many different faiths, including Krishna and the Yoruba *orisha*. Jimi Solanke, one of the country's best-known actors, and Niyi Coker appeared as Godspeak, while Laide Adewole and Funso Alabi, whom I praised for his performance in Bullock's *Road*, played a total of three parts, including Semuwe and Eleazar. This tripling may have been part of a scheme to enable the actors to display their versatility, but it may have been to show how completely Eleazar had, like Brother Jero before him, out-manoeuvred his rival. Although the casting seemed to suggest that Godspeak had no chance to escape, the closing moments of the production, in which Godspeak attacked Eleazar with a cutlass, may have offered some hope: Godspeak finally had the courage to challenge his persecutor physically. Though in some ways a grotesque figure of fun, he, like others before him, fought back and earned respect for so doing.

Requiem (1983) was Soyinka's first production of a major new play since *Wonyosi* in 1977 and his first full-length, totally original script since *Horseman* in 1972. Performances were well attended at Ife and elsewhere, but received little critical attention, certainly not as much as the time which had elapsed since *Wonyosi* and *Horseman* should have guaranteed for a full-length Soyinka. The play is not as significant as many expected. The cause of its weakness is to be found in its origin as a radio play and in the absence of a sufficiently substantial target. The exposure of metaphysicians and parapsychologists could, surely, have been achieved more simply and effectively.

Requiem was toured with a series of brief sketches, *Priority Projects*, directed by Soyinka with Chuck Mike as Assistant Director. These carried forward the playwright's campaign against prestige projects, President Shagari and President Shagari's policies. Four 'projects' were attacked; *Festac 77. Green Revolution, Abuja* and *Ethical Revolution*. All were about 'schemes' which involved vast expense, provided opportunities for the corrupt to make money, and were of little benefit to ordinary Nigerians. In the first, which is about the 'cultural jamboree' held during January 1977, Worker is seen digging a pit; when asked by Visitor why he is digging, he gives no good reason. It is, it seems, just a pit, a hole, a 'project'. After Visitor has left, Worker turns around to reveal 'Festac 77' written on the back of his shirt. *Green Revolution*, an attack on an extensively publicised but atrociously mismanaged agricultural scheme, follows a similar pattern. When interest has been aroused, Worker turns round from his labour on another pit to show that his shirt is inscribed 'Green Revolution'.

A variation on the pattern of exchanges and movements is provided in *Abuja*, a sketch directed at the corruption involved in the construction of the new capital city for the country – a project which resulted in many millions of naira disappearing into 'bottomless pits'. the sketch opens with Worker, out of sight, shovelling earth from a particularly deep pit; Second Worker enters and begins to fill in the hole. The two men strike up a rhythm, excavating and filling in at the same rate. Exchanges between Second Worker and Visitor establish that the date is 1981 and make references to particular areas of corruption: for instance, 'low-cost' houses have been constructed and then demolished, and contracts have been awarded and then cancelled. To continue the pattern of previous scenes, Second Worker turns round to reveal 'Abuja' written on his shirt. The lyrics of the songs sung between the sketches formed a significant part of the production and, in idioms of the market place, drove home the lessons. For instance, one verse went:

> Low-cost housing became mass graves
> One man chops while, the other grieves
> As for Abuja, billions dey roll
> And vanish for ever in the Capital Hole.
>
> *(Unlimited Liability Company)*

Soyinka was deeply affronted that Shagari's regime had the temerity to launch an 'Ethical Revolution', an exercise in what he felt to be large scale hypocrisy in which shysters and opportunists cynically manipulated the language of morality and popular revolt. One of the verses linked to the *Ethical Revolution* sketch ran:

> One morning time I wake for my bed
> And the radio say, I sick for my head
> No, make I talk true, de ting wey e mention
> Na something call etika revolution
> Etika revo kin?
>   Etika revolution
> Etika revo how much?
>
> *(Unlimited Liability Company)*

146

This expresses Soyinka's conviction that those who proclaim the Ethical Revolution have absolutely no intention of allowing their lives to be guided by moral principles.

The style in which many of these verses was sung was one Soyinka had already used in *Opera Wonyosi*, a calypso style which drew on the socially conscious songs of the dead Igbo composer, Ijemanze. *Priority Projects* clearly had precedents in revue pieces from the sixties, such as 'The Ballad of Nigerian Philosophy' and 'The Ogby of Gbu', in *Opera Wonyosi* and *Before the Blow-out*, but it was more purposefully spectacular and more directly political. The music could be danced to and the words were easily committed to memory; the sketches were ideal for open air performances.

As the election approached Soyinka, anxious to remind Nigeria of the scandals of the Shagari administration, turned to the gramophone record industry, which is well established in Nigeria. In July 1983 his album 'Unlimited Liability Company', recorded by Tunji Oyelana and the Benders, appeared under the Enwuro label. The title song fills one side of the record and tells the story of a corrupt 'company' which is mismanaged by a 'chairman' who has neither the will nor the ability to control his 'directors'. It is a *chanson à clef*.

Reviewing the record, Yemi Ogunbiyi of the University of Ife wrote: 'As the catalogue of these excesses and failures is brought to an end, the tempo of the piece suddenly gathers steam, culminating in sharp bursts of rhythmically measured notes of

Se mi jeje, se mi je je
Me too want some gari
Share-de-gari, Share-gari
Share-gari, Share-gari
Share-gari etc'.[3]

'Gari' is made from cassava and is a staple food for many Nigerians: it can have the same idiomatic meaning as 'bread'.

Much of the record is in Ijemanze's style. Entitled 'Etika Revo Wetin?' (What is this Ethical Revolution?) it consists of the songs used in *Priority Projects* and looked towards the August polls. The final verse is

Don't let them take you for another ride
Etika revo wetin?
DROP DEAD!

(Unlimited Liability Company)

Soyinka's record was widely reviewed and responses to it were, predictably, along party lines. It was frequently played on radio stations in states led by opposition Governors. The songs were hugely enjoyed and carried Soyinka's campaign into many villages and homes; they became the anthems of the opposition. The success of the songs emphasised what a potent political weapon lyrics are in Nigeria and represented a significant development in Soyinka's efforts to create a distinctive agit-prop style.

Soyinka was deeply distressed by events preceeding the election and by the 'results' which were announced. In September he spoke on the BBC's World Service about the injustices which had been perpetrated and about the possibilities of a coup. Shagari's government moved against those *radio and television stations which had played Soyinka's songs and the playwright himself was put under pressure. In the event, General Muhammadu Buhari's coup of 31 December 1983 transformed the Nigerian political situation. From the beginning of 1984, Soyinka, the outspoken critic of the fallen Shagari enjoyed a special position in public esteem. During the year, in which his fiftieth birthday was celebrated, he completed a film project on which he had been working for some time and a version of *Blues of a Prodigal* was shown in Ife. He also allowed his anti-military *Jero's Metamorphosis* to be performed at Ife and devoted some energy to the production of a play which had been scheduled for performance three years before, *A Play of Giants*.

9
A Play of Giants

Soyinka regarded Idi Amin, who overthrew Milton Obote and began a reign of terror in Uganda during February 1971, as a symptom of an African disease. Using *Transition/ Ch'Indaba*, the Union of Writers of African Peoples and the Nigerian press, he waged a fierce campaign against the bloody tyranny in Uganda from the mid-seventies. In May 1979, he published a particularly densely textured and carefully structured celebration of the tyrant's downfall, entitled 'Happy Riddance'. The whole gruesome Ugandan sequence, from Amin's rise to power, through his man-ipulation of black opinion and his posturing as a revolution-ary leader to his downfall, scattered lessons which, in Soyinka's opinion, the continent had to learn. In 'Happy Riddance', he wrote:

An all-African commission must sit for an entire year if need be, taking evidence and educating the world yet again on the terrible price paid by ordinary human beings for the illusion of power, and the conspiracy of silence among the select club of leaders.

We are tired of the lies of the past eight years, lies with which the minds of Africans – and black peoples in America and the Caribbean have bent to accommodate a sadist, mass murderer, an incompetent administrator and political buffoon as a hero for black emulation.[1]

Elsewhere in his newspaper articles, Soyinka described Amin as an 'overlarge child', a 'murderous buffoon', 'the tool of neo-imperialist designs' and 'a survivalist killer'. In the same articles he inveighed against the 'smug, comfortable, secure, chauvenistic, self-persuaded radicals' whom he confronted with the gory, gibbering reality of Amin and, an important point, with the reality of other Amins, other tyrants, who held sway in Africa, arranged for opponents to 'disappear' and survived because the people were cowed and cowardly.

Idi Amin, in the person of Kamini, bestrides *A Play of Giants*. A monstrosity who is exposed with a Swiftian attention to repulsive detail, Kamini embodies evil and infuses some of his own daemonic vigour and devilish virulence into Soyinka's play about him – and his like. He is outrageous and brutal, all the more terrifying because based on an identifiable, indeed an easily recognised, original. The play continues to have relevance because, although Amin has been forced into the background, Aminism, a particularly vicious form of Kongism, has not been eliminated.

A Play of Giants was, unlike the agit-prop sketches which immediately preceded it, written for production in a well-equipped theatre building. It was scheduled for performance at Yale University during 1981/82, postponed, and published in 1984 with a note indicating that it would be presented at Yale during 1985. The delays in production had the effect of dimming memories of Amin, and of bringing to the fore the question: why was Amin able to fool so many people about so many things for so long?

A Play of Giants takes place in the Bugaran Embassy 'a few years before the present.' The set represents a magnificent first-floor room, with a wide, sweeping, stone stairway, a curving gallery, a gilt balcony and a view through trees to the United Nations Building in New York. This is strange territory for Soyinka, who had not set a play outside Africa since 1960 and who had, generally, avoided restricting himself to a single, indoor location. The UN Building is intended to place the play precisely; 'we' are in an actual metropolis, close to a centre of power and hope. The Bugaran Embassy, on the other hand, is the product of dramatic licence: there is no such place as Bugara, no such embassy as Soyinka describes. However, Bugara clearly stands for Uganda, and as *A Play of Giants* unfolds the ornate embassy provides a constant and elegant contrast with the barbarous, vulgar viciousness of 'the giants' who swagger through it.

The play opens on Benfacio Gunema (a thinly disguised representation of Macias Nguemo of Equatorial Guinea), Emperor Basco (Jean-Bedel Bokassa of the Central African Empire, a sketch to set beside Boky in *Opera Wonyosi*) and Field-Marshal Kamini (Amin). Attended by a sycophantic Scandinavian journalist, Gudrum, they pose in throne-like chairs for a Sculptor. Their talk of subversives and the suppression of rebellions provides a background to the play and touches on issues which erupt into the foreground when defections are reported, escapes attempted and news of a coup in Bugara arrives. In the opening 'brotherly' exchanges, the Heads of

State reveal their paranoia, ignorance, confusion and stomach-turning ruthlessness while the Sculptor toils away at the group portrait of them and the work of the Embassy continues.

The play retains contact at all points with the 'boulevard', dialogue, single set, two-act tradition of drama. There is no dancing, no music, no flash-back; there are none of the characteristics of either African Festival Theatre or of the latter-day Absurdists to 'disturb' a conservative western or westernised audience. *A Play of Giants* is, however, sub-titled in some scripts 'a fantasia on the Aminian theme' and the action becomes increasingly outrageous and extravagent as the day on which it is set progresses.

The opening exchange between the Heads of State is interrupted by the arrival of the Chairman of the Bugara Central Bank with the news that the World Bank has refused to grant Bugara a huge, outright loan. Kamini's intemperate reply includes the following:

> Let World Bank tell us once and for all if it is just for rich countries and neo-colonial bastards like Hazena or if it belong to Third World countries who need loan (*A Play of Giants*, p.6).[2]

He orders the Chairman to 'get back to Bugara right away and start printing more Bugara bank notes' – a command which further exposes his ignorance and incompetence. The encounter with the Chairman continues with Kamini exhibiting his arrogant brutality: when the banker tells him that Bugaran 'currency is not worth its size in toilet paper', he describes him as 'a syphilitic bastard talking worse than imperialist propaganda' and sentences him 'to eat shit'. A Task Force Special (officer) drags the Chairman into a lavatory which opens onto the set and forces his head into

the lavatory bowl both before and after Kamini has used it.
The audience is reminded of the Chairman's punishment
from time to time during the First Part of the play as the
Task Force Special flushes the cistern over the honest
man's head. The whole, lingering, distasteful episode
illustrates one of the milder, but degrading, ways in which
tyrants such as Kamini punish those who have the temerity
to speak even a fraction of the truth.

Shortly after the Chairman has been dealt with the
Bugaran Ambassador to the United Nations enters 'almost
apologetically'. She announces that she has found the
perfect location for the group monument to African
brotherhood which the Sculptor is creating: the Delegates'
Passage in the UN Building. The question of the fate of the
monument, which contributes both to the plot and the
symbolic quality of the play, further reveals Kamini's
conceit, ignorance, arrogance and philistinism.

The plot, however, is slender and the play's focus is
found in satire and theme rather than action. Between the
rather crudely arranged departures and arrivals, Soyinka
looses satirical shafts at the leaders who flank Kamini. On
one side sits the fascist Gunema with his Spanish interpolations and his admiration of Franco. On the other, the vain,
culturally alienated Gaullist, Kasco, who proclaims that 'to
know French is to understand history' (11) and who
obviously delights in occasions of great splendour.
Soyinka, incidentally, requires that the actors performing
this play adopt a diversity of accents, but the lines he
provides for them show little evidence of close attention to
the varieties of English spoken by, say, Scandinavians,
Russians or Ugandans. His ear for the different kinds of
English spoken in Nigeria is, on the evidence of his writing
to date, much sharper than his ear for the ways in which

English is spoken world-wide. A greater attention to idiom would have improved the play.

The next to enter is another of the giants who give the play its title, Barra Tuboum, whose appearance recalls that of Mobutu Sese Seko of Zaire, makes a flamboyant entrance

> *. . . dressed in a striped animal skin 'Mao' outfit with matching fez-style hat. He sports an ornately carved ebony walking-stick. At his waist is strapped an ivory-handled side-arm stuck in a holster which is also made of zebra skin. (A Play of Giants, p. 18)*

Barra Tuboum launches into an account of his 'campaign to eliminate all foreign influences' (he changed the names on his father's grave) and – making his contribution to the discussion of power and responsibility – of his military action, with the help of French paratroops, against 'the tribe of Shabira'. The account calls to mind Mobutu's dependence on European forces in the Shaba Province of Zaire and exposes the double standards operated by both Tuboum and Mobutu in relation to 'authenticity'. In this instance, as in several others, the reality Soyinka is concerned with is – or was – so bizarre that the satirist's task is not so much that of inventor as of reporter. Mobutu is transformed by means of a few artisitic touches into Barra Tuboum, a 'cowboy' from wildest Central Africa, a clown who is utterly inconsistent in cultural and political matters. The problem faced by the director and actor is how to make Tuboum sinister as well as ridiculous.

Tuboum is given a bare five minutes centre stage before being moved over to make room for the Honourable Mayor of Hyacombe, who comes to shower praises on Kamini and to offer him, as a leader who has given black people 'pride of race', the freedom of Hyacombe. The Mayor, naïve, trusting and black, is accompanied by Professor Batey, who plays a larger role in the events which follow and who is guilty of greater betrayals. An eloquent academic who later shows considerable presence of mind, Batey is one of those who has helped, in the image used in 'Happy Riddance', to *bend* 'the minds of Africans, and black peoples in America and the Caribbean . . . to accommodate a sadist, mass murderer, an incompetent administrator and political buffoon as a hero for black emulation.' Batey is blinded and deafened by his proximity to Power, as embodied in Kamini: he puts his relationship with the tyrant above his loyalty to his old and valued Bugaran friends. Furthermore, he is one of those, frequently castigated by Soyinka, who excuses tyranny on environmental or behaviourist grounds, one of those sophists with sponges who are always found among the camp followers of the powerful. Batey conspicuously fails to display, or even to appreciate, those qualities which Soyinka repeatedly recommends in his prose and which emerge from *A Play of Giants* as virtues. These include: the need to struggle for human rights, the responsibility of the individual for his own actions, the value of friendship and the need to seek out and speak out the truth if 'the man' is not to die.

Towards the end of Part One, Soyinka returns to the question of the destination of the sculpture and increases the tension. The Sculptor reveals that he knows nothing of the plan to put his work in the UN Building. He has, it seems, been commissioned to work on the monument so that a wax-model can be made of it for Madame Tussaud's African exhibition in London. He is perceptive enough to realise that the Chamber of Horrors would be an appropriate setting and incautious enough to share his perception with Gudrum.[3] Kamini is immediately told and puts the 'common Makongo carver' firmly in his place; when the Sculptor attempts to escape he is thwarted and beaten. The embassy which had, at the beginning of the play, looked like a temporary studio, has, by the end of Part One, become a prison. This development anticipates its transformation during the second half of the play into a fortress.

In Part Two, work on the monument continues, only now the Sculptor is bandaged or bound. New satirical targets are wheeled into range and the fantastic element in the play becomes more pronounced. The arrival of the Secretary–General of the UN and of Russian and American delegates ensures that the position of the UN in Africa and the involvement of the world powers in establishing and supporting Kamini emerges. Forces outside Africa, Soyinka makes clear, had used Kamini as a 'tool' for their neo-imperialist designs: they enabled him to torture, maim, terrorise and slaughter 'his' people. Kamini's 'reversal of fortune' comes quickly and decisively – a report of a coup in Bugara reaches the bickering delegates and signals that the pragmatic Russians have no more use for their instrument. The news triggers a characteristically violent response from Kamini: some of the arms supplied by the Russians and Americans for use against Bugarans are, with a twist powered by dramatic justice, pointed at delegations; a rocket-launcher, smuggled into the country with diplomatic baggage, is installed in the lavatory and, as the curtain comes down, Kamini commands his men to fire at the UN Building. This cataclysm is in a very different mood from the intrigues, the jockeying for position, the political one-upmanship and the name-calling which has preceded it; it represents the fullest manifestation of the 'fantasia element'. The 'great powers' had sown the wind; Kamini makes them – or at least New Yorkers and the UN – reap his whirlwind.

A Play of Giants is a virtuoso satirical display written in bile and blood. Kamini is outrageous, an extravagant creation who tugs at the restraints which keep him within a relatively 'well-made play' and seems about to link arms with malignant monsters such as Albert Jarry's King Ubu. The headlong rush with which Soyinka launches himself against those he despises means that he sometimes leaves his flanks vulnerable to counter attacks. In his determination to expose the blinkered selfishness of Kamini's financial 'policy', for instance, he leaves unquestioned the role of the World Bank. In his haste to make fun of the Central Intelligence Agency, he glosses over that organisation's role in Africa. But these nit-picking criticisms are put in perspective by recalling that we do not go to the theatre to listen to discourses on the pros and cons of devaluation, and that we do not go to a Soyinka play for scrupulously balanced accounts of great power involvement in Africa. Soyinka, and this is a quality that informs much of his academic writing as well as his plays, responds viscerally to much that goes on around him. He is here, as so often, debunker not analyst, caricaturist not psychologist, impassioned *provocateur* not detached philosopher.

Yet Soyinka seems to have wanted to make this play a work of some intellectural substance as well as an explosive exposé. *A Play of Giants* contains an intermittently sustained discussion of a theme which has preoccupied Soyinka intellectually for many years: the nature of power and its relationship to responsibility. 'Emperor' Kasco shares his discovery that 'Power comes only with the death of politics'; he maintains that since his coronation he has

risen above intrigue to 'inhabit the pure realm of power'.
(21) Gunema, by contrast, reveals that he searched for
power in the supernatural, particularly in *voodoo*, but only
found it, or, as he says, 'tasted' it, while having sexual
intercourse with a woman who hoped that by sacrificing her
honour she would save her husband's life. Barra Tuboum
has an altogether simpler palate and a more direct means of
satisfying his hunger for power: he relishes fighting, killing
and, finally, eating those who oppose him. He has brought
three prisoners to New York and proposes they be
consumed with cocktails. (18) Kamini has no interest
whatever in abstract issues, no capacity for discussing
power, no aptitude for self-analysis. but, thanks to his Task
Force Specials and the arms at his disposal, he is 'in power'
throughout the play. He brags about the villages and
families he has destroyed in his rage at a single rebel; he
repeats endlessly his barbarous threats ('he will smell his
mother's cunt'); he ensures that the chairman suffers the
punishment he imposes on him ('he will eat shit'). In short,
he 'exercises' power.

The Chairman, the Ambassador, the Mayor, Batey, the
American and Russian Delegates, the Task Force Specials,
the Sculptor, the Secretary-General of the United Nations,
and even the 'rebels' who, in far off Bugara, overthrow
Kamini, all have power of one sort or another. Some use
their power with a sense of responsibility, some do not.
Soyinka, who lists Bertrand Russell's *Power* among those
books which have influenced him and whose nick name at
the University of Ife is the name of his power-crazed leader,
'Kongi', has written a play which contains a series of
pertinent comments on the theme of power and responsibility. As on previous occasions he works through contrasts, comparisons and variations; his own position

emerges only slowly.

A play, any play, certainly *A Play of Giants*, is written to make an impact on audiences, on people. Not in this case, 'the People', if by that term is meant, say, the crowds in African markets and lorry parks, but people who understand English and venture inside theatres, school halls and public meeting places, an international community scattered through Africa, Europe and America. For the benefit of these people Soyinka makes an attack in English which is only slightly indirect and which only the most obtuse can fail to de-code. In choosing this style he knew that the out and out populists would condemn him for addressing 'an elite', that the sophisticated would accuse him of oversimplifying issues and employing crude devices, but that audiences, particularly in Africa, would respond. The English language – as used in the play – can be understood by millions; the bold theatrical and satirical effects can make a deep impact.

The style of the play and the very fact that Soyinka wrote it indicate his desire to communicate and his confidence that audiences – people – can be affected by theatrical experiences. But, while trying to give power *to* the people by making them more alert, Soyinka knows that power does not at present, in Africa, come *from* the people. Power, as *A Play of Giants* makes clear, comes out of the coffers of bankers, out of the cargo-holds of arms-exporting countries and out of the sky in the form of paratroopers.

A Play of Giants represents an attack on African leaders of unprecedented ferocity and is work of considerable courage. Its scale and its violence compel attention; Soyinka seems to stride among African tyrants past and present, pointing to their excesses, recalling their ill-deeds, and drawing attention to the forces which manipulate them. Through this play written with tears straining at the ducts, manic laughter in the throat and teeth set in a grin of grim defiance, he intended to upset and enrage, to tear the bandages from the wounds of a continent and force people to watch the blood flow. A work of this intensity was necessary to make an impact on 'the smug, comfortable, secure chauvinistic, self-persuaded radicals' – and other victims of Aminian manipulations. It was unlike anything he had written before and, produced soon after his fiftieth birthday, indicates that the time has not yet come for anything approaching a final judgement on the work of Wole Soyinka.

References

1. Brief Life

1. Soyinka has written a number of autobiographical articles and a book about his childhood; he has also spoken about himself in interviews. The account which follows draws on these sources, but it has not been submitted to Soyinka for comment or correction.
2. See James Gibbs, '"The Masks Hatched Out": A Study of Soyinka's Plays in Performance,' *Theatre Research International* (Oxford), 7,3 (1982), pp. 180–206. (Contains a bibliography of reviews of productions of Soyinka's plays.)
3. John Mortimer, *Clinging to the Wreckage* (Harmondsworth: Penguin, 1982), pp. 196–199. Mortimer suggests that Soyinka is an 'Ibo'.
4. See James Gibbs, "Tear the Painted Mask: Join the Poison Stains". A Preliminary Study of Wole Soyinka's Writings for the Nigerian Press.' *Research in African Literatures* (Austin, Texas), 14,1 (1983), pp. 3–44.

2. Sources and Influences

1. The conference was held at University College, Ibadan. For a fuller account of Soyinka's paper see James Gibbs, 'Soyinka's Drama of Essence,' *Utafiti* (Dar es Salaam), 3,2 (1978), 427–440.

References

2. See Joel Adedeji, "Alarinjo": The Traditional Yoruba Travelling Theatre,' in *Theatre in Africa* ed. Oyin Ogunba and Abiola Irele, (Ibadan: University of Ibadan Press, 1978), pp. 27-51.
3. See Ebun Clark, *Hubert Ogunde: The Making of Nigerian Theatre* (Oxford: Oxford University Press, 1979).
4. See James Gibbs, 'The Origins of *A Dance of the Forests*,' *African Literature Today* (London), 8 (1976), pp. 66-71.
5. Brooke Hyde, 'Birthday Honours' *West Africa* (London). 6 August 1984, pp. 1578-9.

3. The Leeds Plays

1. Soyinka spoke about the 'genesis' of this and other plays at a play-making workshop held in Harare during December 1981. I have drawn extensively on that and other statements in describing the background to his writing.
2. See, for instance, 'Three Views of *The Swamp Dwellers*', *Ibadan Magazine* (Ibadan), June 1959, pp. 27-30.
3. In addition to the above see Virginia Browne–Wilkinson, *The Horn* (Ibadan), 2,6 (1959), pp. 10-11.

4. The Independence Plays

1. Dapo Adelugba's close association with Soyinka and his sensitivity as a critic have given his writing on Soyinka particular authority. See, for example, 'Trance and Theatre: The Nigerian Experience' in *Drama and Theatre in Nigeria: A Critical Source Book*, ed. Yemi Ogunbiyi, (Lagos: Nigeria Magazine, 1981), pp. 203-218.
2. 'Wole Soyinka' an interview, *Spear* (Lagos), May, 1966, p. 18. This is one of the most helpful of the shorter interviews which have been published. See also those listed in the bibliography to *Critical Perspectives on Wole Soyinka*, ed. James Gibbs (London, Heinemann, 1981).
3. Robert Fraser, 'Four Alternative Endings of Wole Soyinka's *A Dance of the Forests*,' *Research in African Literatures* (Austin, Texas), 10,3 (Winter, 1979), 359–374. See also Nick Wilkinson, 'Demoke's Choice in Soyinka's *A Dance of the Forests*,' *Journal of Commonwealth Literature* (London), 10,3 (April 1976), pp. 22-27.

4. Peter Enahoro, 'Wole Soyinka Has Overdone it this Time,' *Daily Times* (Lagos), 7 October 1960, p. 5.
5. 'Nigeria's Bernard Shaw,' *Drum* (Lagos), March 1961, p. 27.

5. Plays of the Sixties

1. See Robin Horton, 'New Year in the Delta, A Traditional and a Modern Festival,' *Nigeria Magazine* (Lagos), 67 (December 1960), pp. 256–297, for an illuminating account of a purification festival similar to that held in Eman's 'home town'.
2. *Childe Internationale* is published in *Before the Blackout*, which is unfortunately not easy to obtain.
3. See, once again, the interview in *Spear* magazine, p. 18.
4. Penelope Gilliatt, 'A Nigerian Original,' *The Observer* (London), 19 September 1965, reprinted in *Critical Perspectives on Wole Soyinka*, pp. 106–107.
5. See, for instance, a conference paper by Biodun Jeyifo, 'The Hidden Class Struggle in *The Road*,' presented at Ibadan in 1976.
6. *Spear* magazine, p. 18, Banda's 'Dead-or-Alive Search Order' was reported in *The Times* (London), 29 October 1964.
7. The script for the film differs substantially from the edited and released version of the film. Soyinka has dissociated himself from the version seen on the screen.

6. A Post-War Play

1. Alan Bunce, 'Soyinka's Nigerian Play,' *Christian Science Monitor* (Boston), 15 August 1970.
2. Abiola Irele, 'Portrait of a Catching Sickness,' *Sunday Times* (Lagos), 28 March 1971.

7. Plays of Exile

1. Albert Hunt, 'Amateurs in Horror', *New Society* (London), 9 August 1973, p. 343. The article is reprinted in *Critical Perspectives on Wole Soyinka*.
2. I have incured many debts to students and colleagues during

the time that I have been responding to Soyinka's plays. In a book of this kind there is no space for detailed acknowledgement, but at this point I would like to express my gratitude to Akinade M. Bello, who, while a student at the University of Ibadan, made enquiries into the ritual suicide at Oyo. My account of the sequence of events draws on his unpublished research.

3. D.S. Izevbaye, 'Naming and the Character of African Fiction,' unpublished paper, f.n. 20.

8. Plays for Nigeria of the Seventies and Eighties

1. John Willett. *The Theatre of Bertolt Brecht*, London: Methuen, 1959, pp. 29–30.
2. Biodun Jeyifo, 'Drama and the New Social Order,' *Positive Review* (Ife), (1978), p. 22, and Yemi Ogunbiyi, '*Opera Wonyosi*: A Study of Wole Soyinka's *Opera Wonyosi*,' *Nigeria Magazine* (Lagos), Nos 128/9 (1979), pp. 3–13. Ogunbiyi points out that, in Yoruba, 'opera' means 'the fool buys' – at this point the tonal inflections are very signficant. 'Wonyosi' is an expensive lace.
3. Yemi Ogunbiyi, 'Requiem for a Managing Director,' *The Guardian* (Lagos), August 7, 1983, p. 23.

9. A Play of Giants

1. Wole Soyinka, 'Happy Riddance', *Nigerian Herald*, 25.4.79. See also 'Halt Idi Amin', *Sunday Times* (Lagos), 27.7.75, 'The Inquisition in Uganda', *Sunday Times*, 10.4.77, and various numbers of *Transition*.
2. Page numbers refer to the 1984 Methuen edition. 'Hazena' represents Tanzania, one of the African countries which in Soyinka's opinion has made a resolute attempt to become independent and socialist.
3. Soyinka suggests that the models in Madame Tussaud's Wax Museum are made from sculptures. They are, in fact, not generally made by the methold employed by the Sculptor. The Chamber of Horrors, which contains models of executions, murderers and the like, has often been drawn into remarks and comparisons made by British humourists and would-be humourists.

Bibliography

Plays

Before the Blackout, Ibadan: Orisun, 1971.

Collected Plays I, London: Oxford University Press, 1973. (Contains *A Dance of the Forests, The Swamp Dwellers, The Strong Breed, The Road, The Bacchae of Euripides.*)

Collected Plays II, London: Oxford University Press, 1974. (Contains *The Lion and the Jewel, Kongi's Harvest, The Trials of Brother Jero, Jero's Metamorphosis, Madmen and Specialists.*)

Six Plays, London: Methuen, 1984. (Contains *The Trials of Brother Jero, Jero's Metamorphosis, Camwood on the Leaves, Death and the King's Horseman, Madmen and Specialists, Opera Wonyosi.*)

A Play of Giants, London: Methuen, 1984.
Requiem for a Futurologist, London: Collings, forthcoming.

Other Writings

1957 'Madame Etienne's Establishment,' (short story), *The Gryphon* (Leeds), March, pp. 11–22.

Bibliography

1957 'A Tale of Two Cities,' (short story), *The Gryphon* (Leeds), Autumn, pp. 16–22.

1958 'A Tale of Two Cities,' (a different short story), *New Nigerian Forum* (London), 2 (May), pp. 26–30.

1960 'The Future of African Writing,' (criticism), *The Horn* (Ibadan), 4,1, pp. 10–16.

1962 *Culture in Transition*, (film), Esso World Theatre.

1965 *The Interpreters*, (novel), London: Deutsch.

1966 'And After the Narcissist?', (criticism), *African Forum* (New York), 1,4 (Spring), pp. 53–64.

1966 'Of Power and Change,' (political comment), *African Statesman* (Lagos), 1,3 (July-Sept) pp. 17–19.

1967 *'Idanre' and Other Poems*, London: Methuen.

1968 *The Forest of a Thousand Daemons*, (translation), London: Nelson.

1969 'The Fourth Stage: Through the Mysteries of Ogun to the Origin of Yoruba Tragedy,' (dramatic theory), in *The Morality of Art*, ed. D.W. Jefferson, London: Routledge and Kegan Paul, pp. 119–134.

1972 *A Shuttle in the Crypt*, (poems), London: Collings and Methuen.

1972 'Interviews' in *African Writers Talking* ed. Dennis Duerden and Cosmo Pieterse, London: Heinemann, pp. 169–180.

1972 *The Man Died*, ('prison notes'), London: Collings.

1973 *Season of Anomy*, (novel), London: Collings.

1975 'Drama and the Revolutionary Ideal,' (lecture), in *In Person: Achebe, Awoonor and Soyinka*, ed Karen L. Morell,

Seattle: University of Washington, pp. 61–88. Morell's volume also contains transcripts of discussion and rehearsal sessions with Soyinka.

1975 *Poems of Black Africa*, edited by Soyinka, London: Secker and Warburg.

1975 'Neo-Tarzanism: The Poetics of Pseudo-Tradition,' (article), *Transition* (Accra), 48, pp. 38–44.

1976 *Myth, Literature and the African World*, (lectures), London: Cambridge University Press.

1976 *Ogun Abibimañ*, (epic poem), London: Collings.

1981 *Aké: The Years of Childhood,* (autobiography), London: Collings.

1981 *The Critic and Society: Barthes, Leftocracy, and Other Mythologies*, (inaugural lecture), University of Ife Press.

1983 'Shakespeare and The Living Dramatist,' (conference paper), *Shakepeare Survey* (Cambridge), 36, pp. 1–10.

1983 *Unlimited Liability Company*, (record), Ewuro Productions, Lagos.

1983 'Electoral Fraud and the Western Press,' (political comment), *Index on Censorship* (London), 12,6 (December), pp. 11–14.

1984 *Blues for a Prodigal,* (film), previewed at Ife.

Secondary Sources

Banham, Martin, with Clive Wake, *African Theatre Today*, London: Pitman, 1976.

Banham, Martin, Wole Soyinka's '*The Lion and the Jewel*' London: Collings and the British Council, 1981.

Bibliography

Booth, James, *Writers and Politics in Nigeria*, London: Hodder, 1981.

Chinweizu, Onwuchekwa Jemie and Ihechukwu Madubuike, *Toward the Decolonization of African Literature*, Enugu: Fourth Dimension, 1980.

Dunton, C.P., *Three Short Plays: Wole Soyinka*, Beirut: York, and Harlow: Longman, 1982. (On *The Swamp Dwellers, The Strong Breed* and *The Trials of Brother Jero*. York Notes series.)

Etherton, Michael, *The Development of African Drama*, London: Hutchinson, 1982.

Gibbs, James, ed. *Critical Perspectives on Wole Soyinka*, London: Heinemann, 1981.

Gibbs, James, *"The Lion and the Jewel": Wole Soyinka*, Beirut: York, and Harlow: Longman, 1982. (York Notes series.)

Gibbs, James, *Study Aid to 'Kongi's Harvest'*, London: Collings, 1973.

Graham-White, Anthony, *The Drama of Black Africa*, New York: French, 1974.

Jones, Eldred, *The Writing of Wole Soyinka*, London: Heinemann, 1981.

King, Bruce, ed. *Introduction to Nigerian Literature*, London: Evans, and Lagos: University of Lagos, 1971.

Moore, Gerald, *Wole Soyinka*, London: Evans, 1978.

Lindfors, Bernth, ed. *Critical Perspectives on Nigerian Literatures*, London: Heinemann, 1979.

Lindfors, Bernth, *Early Nigerian Literature*, New York: Africana, 1982.

Ogunba, Oyin, *The Movement of Transition: A Study of the Plays of Wole Soyinka*, Ibadan: Ibadan University Press, 1975.

Ralph-Bowman, Mark, "Leaders and Left-overs"; A Reading of Soyinka's *Death and the King's Horseman*', *Research in African Literatures* (Austin, Texas), 14,1 (Spring 1983), pp. 81–97.

Roscoe, Adrian, *Mother is Gold*, London: Cambridge University Press, 1971.

Schwarz, Walter, *Nigeria*, London: Pall Mall, 1968.

Sekoni, Ropo, 'Metaphor as Basis of Form in Soyinka's Drama,' *Research in African Literatures* (Austin, Texas), 14,1 (Spring 1983) pp. 45–57.

Tripathi, P.D., '*The Lion and the Jewel*': A Comparative and Thematic Approach,' *Ba Shiru* (Wisconsin), 11,1 (1980), pp. 82–101.

Index